BEINGS

AND

DOINGS

An allegory of God's love

S.L. McGREGOR

First published in 2016 by Lightning Source, Inc.,
La Vergne, Tennessee, United States,
a business unit of Ingram Content Group.

Cover by Elif Mokran

ISBN 978-2-9558663-0-6

www.ingramcontent.com

Praise for *Beings and Doings*

It takes creative genius to tell an old and familiar story in a way that gives us eyes to see what we have missed. McGregor has done just that and more. She has given us the eyes of a child. I was mesmerized by this story. It haunted my soul, yet bathed it in wonder. *Beings and Doings* is beautifully written and simple, yet theologically profound and psychologically astute. This is a book that carries the healing care of the Holy Spirit. Brilliant!

— C. Baxter Kruger, Ph.D., theologian and author of the international bestseller, *The Shack Revisited.*

INDEX

Dedication

To my son, for his unflagging faith in me coupled with an astute but remorseless eye for editing.

Chapter 1

Long ago a sparkling mass of liquid turquoise called Glass Ocean encompassed large portions of a planet in a galaxy related to ours. Wafting above it there was always enough breeze to caress the sails of the lone yacht that sliced across its rippled surface. However, if the boat's two crew members, Allmen and Divita, decided to drop anchor, the waters immediately smoothed to crystal stillness, as if the wind's breath was alive and aware.

Though an infinite number of similar, delightful voyages were filed in their memories, and as many more expected, and though Allmen and Divita between them knew many things, both were oblivious to the calamity that lurked unseen on this day.

Allmen and Divita were beautiful, kind, wise, gentle, patient - perfect! They acknowledged their perfection without a trace of pride. It was simply who and how they were. Their home was the lush island of Being-by-Seeing, where soft beaches resembling frills of golden lace edged deep emerald lagoons. The mountains and hills were cloaked in velvety green grass, and when a puff of cloud draped itself over a peak, like a wig of white hair, well, Being-by-Seeing could truly be called well-dressed.

Hundreds of miles across the waters, the desolate land of Striving-to-Become baked under a merciless darkened sun which, despite its heat, emitted little light.

Apart from Allmen and Divita there were no human Beings in either of these places, though multitudes of animals, reptiles, birds and fish lived happily together - except for one unpleasant jellyfish called Big-Ego. He was the only inhabitant of Striving-to-Become, and he didn't belong anywhere else.

Big-Ego was, in fact, King of Striving-to-Become, but there isn't much point in being a king if there's no one to rule over. Day after day Big-Ego set off from the desert shallows and roamed the ocean, hoping to find and capture slaves in his long tentacles that hung like tresses of shiny, silvery hair from his transparent body. He looked quite gorgeous - at least until closer inspection exposed the sticky lassos hiding in that mane, waiting to entangle and glue up any unfortunate prey. He was like a huge, translucent spider that dragged its own living web behind itself.

Big-Ego's gummy arsenal glistened and gleamed and reflected light like a multifaceted sea-jewel, like a captured and devoured rainbow. He appeared beautiful, and he flaunted this beauty. And he was very, very dangerous, which fact he concealed.

Big-Ego billowed his stomach and undulated the ridges that lined his amorphous shape like combs. He slid forward through the deep blue - and smashed into the invisible Wall. His eyes, all twenty four of them, rolled up in his head as he spiraled down, and down. He regained consciousness in depths he preferred never to visit - though not because of any lurking danger, for there was no danger anywhere except where he brought it himself.

No, he detested all places that had a shortage of light, because then he was forced to observe himself without any refracted glory and, in the gloom, see himself as he really was - a formless, ugly glob with no attractive assets of his own. He could reflect and hide beneath a prism of colors, but in himself there was only the shapeless emptiness of a total absence of light. His good looks, like his personality, were based on deception.

The Wall, he thought, shaking his head to clear it. *The stupid Wall.*

The only thing he hated more than the Wall was the one he blamed for its construction, the Builder. Big-Ego was so blinded by pride he didn't realize that he himself was responsible for its creation. As his internal eyesight had dimmed along with the sun of Striving-to-Become, so the Wall had grown until it reached the surface and obstructed his way forever. But it was his own darkened vision of the Builder that had raised it, block by unbelieving block.

After another shiver and shake of long tentacles he shot upwards, becoming more splendid with every yard closer to the light-filled surface. Bitterness twisted his large mouth, but in the sun's bouncing rays it looked as if he were smiling. Busy with his temper, he smashed through the sea's shining crust into the shimmering air above…and heard a tinkling voice.

'Darling, look! What is it? It's beautiful!'

Big-Ego rolled in the water, trying to hide, the sour taste of fear bitter on his tongue.

He'd never seen a yacht. It was like a hovering monster with enormous white, flapping wings, carrying two creatures so covered in radiance that he couldn't be sure what they looked like. But he recognized their flaming glow: it was the same glory that robed the Builder. It was the same glory that he himself had once worn proudly...too proudly.

Therefore these living torches were enemies - prey. But they probably didn't know this as clearly as he did. He'd sensed their existence during the numberless eons of his exile, but it seemed that they didn't recognize him. He slithered closer, crinkling the water so that it reflected even more sunlight off him, dazzling his onlookers.

'Ooh! What are you?' Divita asked, her voice light with laughter.

'A box jellyfish,' Allmen answered, a smile in his rich baritone - before Big-Ego had time to open his mouth. The jellyfish narrowed all of his two dozen eyes, which also helped shield them from the glare pouring off the luminous human Beings. He wondered how the male of the species knew.

No time for that now, he thought, his mind hurtling through plans.

All the while the jellyfish was thinking he gyrated and flexed to show off his borrowed colors - until he felt the water around the motionless yacht heating up from the Beings' glow. And that was a problem.

Big-Ego scooted away, hunting for a cooler spot. As he passed the boat's stern he saw the rudder hanging beneath the hull, connected by some kind of cylindrical post. Instantly a scheme formed in his mind.

The yacht must have sailed either across or through the Wall; perhaps the Wall stops at the surface, or maybe it doesn't affect the glory-coated human Beings. Perhaps I can cross it too, if I'm attached to the yacht...? Under their cover?

If I can get to the island from where I was banished then maybe, maybe I'll find a way to steal back some of my lost glory. He wanted that more than anything in existence. He'd murder, pillage, rob, torture, do whatever was necessary unhesitatingly, if it would restore the longed-for glory. And if it didn't, then Plan

B would involve having some company in his dark and empty lostness.

Okay, Big-Ego thought, *it's worth a try.* He wrapped several tentacles around the rudder's post, making sure he was hidden from view by the overhanging transom. From this position he could hear the conversation from the deck, and the water was cooler.

'The jellyfish must be the shy type,' Divita said, searching the sea with eyes the color of the brooks that bubbled across the island - or so Allmen thought whenever he looked at her.

'It was a ctenophore; they reflect like a faceted diamond,' he said.

'You know so much, sometimes I'm in awe of you.' Divita looked at her husband with such open admiration that Allmen blushed.

'No, my love,' he said, smiling. 'Remember, the Builder shared his knowledge between us, so that together we can have the joy of constant discovery of each other – and through each other. I'm just the one who happens to know about sea creatures!'

Allmen draped his arm across his beloved's shoulders as he, too, scanned the water for the missing jellyfish; then his gaze drifted to the horizon. He jumped to his feet, swinging the tiller at the same time; the always-available wind caught at the floppy sails, filling them. The yacht picked up speed, raising a frothing wake.

'What's wrong, darling?' Divita asked, seeing Allmen's frown and the set lines around his strong mouth.

'We've sailed more days than I noticed,' he answered. 'Don't bother to look, it's not worth seeing, but I glimpsed land. It must be Striving-to-Become. I shouldn't have let us get this close, since the Builder warned us that going there would kill us.'

'No, the Builder said we'd die. Is that the same as not existing anymore?'

'I – I don't think so. I'm a bit hazy in that area. I sense that it has something to do with no longer knowing the Builder. Anyway, if he doesn't want us to go there, that's enough for me.'

'Mmm. Me too. Look at that cloud formation, isn't it lovely?'

Even over the sound of the gurgling wake, Big-Ego heard every word. The first seeds of a plan sowed themselves in his murky brain.

'Yes!' he whispered, curling a free tentacle into a fist and shaking it. Again something about the shape of his mouth resembled a smile, however remotely. 'I might be able to get more than a bit of glory back - I might get the Island, and a couple of slaves as well! I might get it all!'

He would have laughed if he could remember how.

It took several days to sail back to the Island of Being-by-Seeing, and Big-Ego hung on doggedly all the way. The closer they came to it, the more his excitement increased. He smelled afresh the forgotten fragrance of air laden with the scents of exotic plants, air so full of life it made him nauseous.

At last they dropped anchor in a deep, lush bay. The two glowing humans walked ashore on the water, sometimes diving into it and racing each other, and laughing, laughing until Big-Ego thought he'd vomit.

Only when they were a fair distance away could Big-Ego look at them without hurting his eyes. Their brightness was going to be a problem.

But I'll make a plan, he thought. *There's always a way.*

The glow was stronger when they were together - a reason to separate them. Big-Ego knew that the glow emanated from the presence of the Builder inside them, of which they were permanently and happily aware.

The human Beings lived at the top of the

beach, beneath two coconut palms. There was no need of further shelter in the perfect climate. The sand was a soft mattress, and since there weren't any neighbors, privacy wasn't a problem. It was easy for Big-Ego to hear them chatting to each other while he skulked in the shallows. And how they talked, all day long!

Envy gobbled at the jellyfish like a hungry whale that had once almost slurped him up with a school of plankton. He hadn't had anyone to converse with since he was cast out, almost too long ago to remember.

There was another problem as well - how to stay unseen while he patrolled the ultra-clear water. Great care was needed.

That evening, as the sun colored the sky different gemstone hues before it sank out of sight, Big-Ego wondered if it had gone off-course and started to rise again, because the Island began to pulsate with light. But the increasing radiance was brighter than the sun...

Oh, no! It must be the Builder! All of a sudden he remembered how the Builder had at times, somehow, appeared outside as well as inside of himself, Big-Ego. *Before that was my name.*

The Builder strode across the beach like a swirling whirlwind of light that glowed with a deep hum, as of words being spoken continuously - or perhaps sung. As Allmen and Divita rushed forward to be embraced in a mighty hug, the Island's air thickened like buttery cream, pulsating with intermingled peace and joy that vibrated in tune with the Beings' heartbeats in such harmony that they felt united with creation, with the universe itself, all contained within the Builder.

Big-Ego scooted frantically back to the slight cover of the hull. He had forgotten how bright and searingly hot the Builder's glow was when he manifested his presence. The water temperature felt close to boiling. Big-Ego wished the ocean would suck him out and hide him in its depths; the brightness was blinding him - melting him - he had to get away - he was being annihilated by glory –
'Aaahh!! Aaaaaaarghh!!!'

He had never swum faster, never but once been more afraid than in those minutes before his frenzied escape to the ocean proper.

Many days passed before Big-Ego's shriveled body re-hydrated, days during which he stayed far from the Island he both detested and desired. Days in which his hatred grew, glowing black as burnished tar as it fed on memories of how good his life had once been.

Well, he thought, ***my*** *glory is improving daily, too - the un-glory of absolute darkness.* It deepened with his growing hate, and he coated himself in it, and drew it round him. When it was thick enough to conceal and maybe even protect him - he hoped - he turned towards the Island and began his return journey. He was more dangerous than ever because the plan to regain what he had lost was taking shape.

Big-Ego roamed the shoreline waters for weeks or months - it was hard to keep track of time when every day was as blissful as the one before and the one to come. Blissful, that is, if you weren't a jellyfish named Big-Ego. For him they were monotonously similar: dreary with a too-bright sun and depressing with happiness. His cloak of bitterness and envy and resentment cut him off from all that was good and beautiful around him. The tension of staying alert for the Builder's return was an added strain.

Big-Ego finally made contact with the Beings, who soon considered him a special pet. He crooned sweet nonsense from the shallows, but now and then he slipped in a little drop of poison, perhaps about the Builder being too dazzling, or parading his glory coat too obviously.

'He needs to tone it down, not show it off,' the jellyfish sang, and moved swiftly on to a harmless ditty before they could remonstrate. And if he found one of the Beings alone he'd quickly sow musical colors of mistrust between them, and include the Builder.

'Oh, Allmen,' he'd serenade sweetly, 'don't you think, *tra-la-la*, that the Builder has graced Divita with a deeper appreciation of beauty than he gave you? Maybe she's extra-special to him, *tra-la*.' Or he'd hum to Divita, 'Why did the Builder make Allmen so much stronger than you? He must think you're less worthy.'

Slowly, imperceptibly, the glory-glow surrounding the Builder began to dim in the Beings' eyes, just a fraction, hardly noticeable, as their trusting innocence was daily tarnished. Big-Ego found Divita's extraordinary innocence a tougher challenge. He decided to focus more energy on her.

He stalked her when she swam, and tied his tendrils to the rudder whenever they went sailing, but Allmen was always too near for him to make a move on her.

The longed-for opportunity arrived when the yacht was again far from the Island - possibly across the invisible Wall. Cloaked as he was in his fug of personal darkness, it was impossible for Big-Ego to tell. Divita was at the helm, chatting to Allmen as usual, when her tinkling laugh rang out. It sounded to Big-Ego's ears like crashing thunder, which worked as a wake-up call, for he'd dozed off. When he realized that Divita was laughing at Allmen's snores, he went into action.

'Hello-o-o, beau-u-ti--ful l-a-a-ady,' he trilled, dropping his sinister cloak and hooking it over the rudder. He did have a most magnificent tenor voice, reaching high C notes without faltering, and, uniquely, he even had some vocal chords that sounded like instruments. So when he pushed out from the

hull, rolling in the sunlight and reflecting myriad colors while imitating a full orchestra, Divita was quite as enthralled as he'd intended she be.

'Oh,' she said softly, so as not to spoil Allmen's sleep. 'You really are simply gorgeous! And your voice - amazing!'

That comment went down well, but for once Big-Ego had more important things on his mind than his big ego. He sang another aria that tugged at Divita's gentle nature, softening her heart towards the seemingly harmless and happy troubadour from the depths.

'Oh, my! Where did you learn to sound like that?' she asked, enchanted, as the last treble trembled in the air.

'In the land of Striving-to-Become, of course,' Big-Ego said with a simper, managing to concoct what looked like an innocent smile. His plan depended on convincing this human who already had everything from the Builder, that she didn't have everything. It was going to be like persuading her that she wasn't on the yacht she was on, but that she must instead go searching for it. It was the most gigantic lie he'd ever attempted, but after all he was the best, a self-taught master of the art of deception.

For he had to get Divita to believe at least one 'I-am-not' from his loaded arsenal: either that she didn't possess the Builder's glory - with which she was actually saturated - or that she could get more of it, or a better quality of it, by earning it herself instead of marinating in it freely as she now did. Her glory was the Builder's, a perfect reflection of his love and beauty as seen clearly through the eyes of her understanding, but the moment she believed she lacked it, she'd begin the never-ending journey of striving to regain it, and she would keep on trying, and on, and on. He knew that from personal experience…

'Striving-to-Become? Divita said, crinkling her lovely forehead and interrupting the jellyfish's rosy musings. 'You mean that place where we're not supposed to go?'

Now Big-Ego had his cue. 'Not supposed to go there? Dear, beautiful, lovely lady, why ever not? It's abso-lute-ly wonderful, the original DIY land - that means do-it-yourself - and once you've worked for something, such as being good, and earned it, there's such satisfaction as you can't imagine!' He shook a gleaming tentacle at Divita, showering her in cool, glowing droplets of water.

From seemingly nowhere a succession of thoughts slithered into Divita's mind. *I am lacking something. Therefore I am not perfect after all. I need to be better, so that I can be good enough for Allmen, and for the Builder. **I am not** yet good enough.* It was a disturbing sequence that shook the foundation of her self-image.

The jellyfish saw his I-am-not hook lodge deep. She was perfect in every way, but she was no longer certain of it. *Hah!* If he could get her to work at being good, to earn goodness instead of just resting in *being* good, then – then – then she would be acting independently of the Builder, and straightaway she'd *feel* separated from him, though that would be only in her mind. When she felt separated she'd experience first, fear, then she'd panic about being abandoned, and then guilt would follow as she thought she was the cause of the problems and she'd think she needed to be punished. After that, victory was his.

All this the simpering jellyfish knew, having been there and done it.

Bewilderment clouded Divita's gentle eyes, dulling their sparkle. She glanced towards her sleeping partner. Big-Ego jumped quickly into action.

'This is exactly what the Builder is keeping from you! For some strange, selfish reason he doesn't want you to experience the joy of earning your own way, of growing to maturity independently. He wants to keep you harnessed to himself, never knowing all there is to know, never even knowing about working to become good! Doesn't that bother you? Don't you realize *you are not* yet grown up?'

Now Divita's eyes flashed. 'Mr. Jellyfish! Really! The Builder's not like that! I don't think you've met him, or you wouldn't say such things!' The sensation of anger was a new experience, one which Divita didn't like. She stared, perplexed, at the lovely creature in the water below and tried to process the tumult of alien thoughts and emotions he'd generated in her.

There was, too, an unfamiliar sensation of coldness in a tiny part of her stomach, as if a dank little well had been dug into it. Though small, it had a sense of bottomlessness that she feared would suck her in if she peered too closely. She looked up, thinking a cloud had floated across the sun, but the sky was clear, though it seemed fractionally dimmer.

She shook her head as if to dispel the strange impressions. *Of course the jellyfish is well-intentioned*, she thought. Suspicion was as foreign to her as envy or jealousy or dislike or bitterness or strife, so she had no armor against it.

Big-Ego could almost follow her musings. It was time to distract her again.

'Hey, lady! I mean, er, dear lovely lady, could you turn down the light a bit? I usually, y'know, keep my eyes below water; your glory-glow's getting to me.' Lacing some truth into a lie always helped - he really was beginning to suffer. The water was definitely warming too, though slightly less than before, he noticed smugly.

'I'm sorry, I can't help it! What shall I do?' Divita was mortified that she could cause discomfort to anybody.

'Nothing, there's nothing you can do.' Big-

Ego said, desperately uncomfortable with the increasing temperature. *Not yet anyway!* 'Yes, well, guess it's time to go then. I'll get back to you another day, okay?'

'Oh! Yes, that would be lovely. Thank you for your songs. Goodbye.'

Big-Ego dived down to a cooler level so quickly that his spidery tentacles flicked spumes of froth into the air. Already the outer layer of his transparent skin was wrinkled by the flames of Divita's glory that seared the sea's surface. He looked and felt half-baked.

Deep down though he was, he faintly made out Allmen's voice from the deck above:

'Mmm. I must have dozed off. Were you saying something to me?'

'No, dearest, I was talking to that delightful creature, the jellyfish. He's a darling, and has the most amazing tenor voice; this time he sang like a full orchestra. I hope you'll hear it too, some day.'

'I look forward to it, my love.' If Allmen had seen the evil grin plastered across the face many fathoms beneath him, he would certainly have changed his mind.

More days passed, and then weeks, during which Big-Ego waited, and watched, and listened. At first he'd thought that Divita was sweet but stupid. Now he realized that she was merely innocent; her knowledge was only of goodness and beauty and love, and it coated her protectively. Allmen, he found, was less naïve, able to process information and store it in mental files - which made him an easier target. The jellyfish fed him a diet of tainted information to categorize – after considered analysis. Allmen trashed most of it, but a few juicy titbits made it into the archives of his mind.

Big-Ego then focused his attention on Divita, though he sang an occasional song or put on a light display for both the Beings, just often enough not to raise Allmen's suspicions. During hours of harmless conversation with Divita he sometimes planted only a tiny seed of discord or distrust or disloyalty; but sometimes more than one. As time flowed by Divita grew fond of the ubiquitous, tentacled minstrel.

Slowly, slowly, the weed-seeds sprouted.

Divita began to think about the wonderful

land of Striving-to-Become, where she would experience the satisfaction of working to become everything she already was but thought she wasn't. At first it hadn't quite made sense, but because she had no experience of lies, she believed that everything Big-Ego said was true. Though she and Allmen shied away from talking openly about the strange but alluring foreign land, their unity of mind and heart enabled her to sense his interest.

Chapter 3

And so a day arrived when Big-Ego sang and chatted, and helped steer the yacht - as he now often did by controlling the rudder from under the water - and distracted the humans from Being-by-Seeing. He talked them into snooze-mode before they noticed the thin dark line of Striving-to-Become on the far horizon. Soon Big-Ego had maneuvered the vessel so close to land that the desert's sand dunes were clearly visible, even against the deep azure shadows formed by the hot, dark sky.

Big-Ego slid a slimy tentacle up the hull and felt for Divita. She woke with a start.

'Sshh!!' whispered Big-Ego. 'Look! There's the fabled, forbidden land that you are afraid of. Not so scary after all, is it?'

Both from the unaccustomed lack of moisture in the air, and because of her fear, Divita's throat was so dry she could hardly speak.

'But-' she said, croaking like an old woman, though that was a concept she couldn't conceive of either. "We mustn't – I mean, we mustn't -'

'Tut, tut, dear girl. Take a good look. Nothing bad there. Actually, I think it's spectacular, all that sand piled up into mountains, rather amazing. No life to be seen anywhere, nothing to be afraid of. See?' He'd picked his words. Much better to say, 'No life anywhere,' than 'Death everywhere.' He swallowed a giggle at his cleverness, and tasted the nickname he'd hit upon for his kingdom: *I-am-Not Land.*

Divita peeked. Big-Ego was right. The land looked strange and different, rather dim, but she didn't see anything there to be afraid of.

'Now,' said Big-Ego, 'we both know Allmen wouldn't want you to explore - he's such a controlling personality, you poor dear. But if you're quiet, we can swim ashore and take a look. Then you'll be doing something for yourself, and earning your right to self-expression. After all, you aren't Allmen's slave; you do have rights, you know.'

Under the spell of Big-Ego's musical voice Divita quite forgot that it wasn't Allmen who didn't want them having anything to do with Striving-to-Become, it was the Builder - the Builder who loved them and wanted to protect them.

'Alright,' Divita said in a croaking whisper. 'But you go ahead; the water will get too hot for you when I get in.'

'Too right,' said Big-Ego, dilating his stomach and body combs and moving quickly towards the beach. Divita watched, quelling a rising panic. She longed to wake Allmen. *But I'm not a little girl anymore. I must become more independent of Allmen and the Builder. They want to control me. That's because **I am not** fully mature yet.*

Although the jellyfish couldn't hear her thoughts, her body-language gave her away. As he read her, excitement rippled through him as if his chords had been struck with a rock.

Listening to Big-Ego's endless flow of insinuations had dulled the eyes of Divita's mind so that her mental picture of the Builder was out of focus, whereas the ideas planted by the jellyfish were in sharp detail.

Feeling emotionally mangled, and with gooseflesh rising from an increasingly noticeable wind that seemed to be cuddling her alone, she decided to stop thinking and just act. Taking a breath, she dived in and swam to a point some distance from Big-Ego. Her feet touched the bottom and she scrambled ashore, half-expecting who-knows-what to happen, for the turmoil wringing her insides was now too strong to ignore. Something was wrong, though she didn't understand yet what 'wrong' was. It was more like, not-right, this choosing her way over the Builder's; this doubting his trustworthiness. This dizzying, hollow feeling of 'I am not.'

She climbed up the slope and felt the hot sand squish between her toes – and that was all. Nothing happened.

Nothing that she noticed at first.

Her glory shimmered and flamed as always while she skipped across the boiling beach on tip-toes. The heat was overpowering. *No wind here,* she thought. If she had but glanced around then she would have seen the desert clearly, its stark dark emptiness exposed by her light - but instead she made a flying leap, giggling with mixed relief and tension, back into the cooler sea.

The sound woke Allmen. He sat up, looked around, saw the dunes, realized that his wife was missing, and experienced the fear of loss for the first time ever. When he heard her voice calling to him from the land, his relief was stronger than his initial anger.

'Darling,' Divita shouted, waving, feeling terribly alone. 'Come! There's nothing here, it's alright, I've even walked on the beach. The Builder must have been mistaken; maybe he's never been here. There's no danger, unless you're scared of hot sand! Come, join me!' She forced gaiety into her words, but she was pretending – a gut reaction of panic. Every word, every moment, every breath of this strange land's empty air felt as if it dragged Allmen further from her, as though he was receding down a long tunnel.

Meanwhile, Big-Ego was utterly devastated. Divita was right - nothing had happened to her. He couldn't believe it, couldn't understand it. How was it possible? She had agreed to try to become what she thought she was not, by setting foot on the land of Striving-to-Become, the land he, Big-Ego had caused to exist by committing the same egotistical crime - and she wasn't punished. It wasn't right; it wasn't fair!

A heartbeat later he understood what had occurred. Allmen and Divita were united; the two had become one. It was as if their union straddled the gap between the yacht and the beach, one foot on each. Therefore, until Allmen added his agreement to the decision - his half making the union whole again - nothing would happen!

With every ounce of himself Big-Ego cursed the Builder's passion for union. Bile slid up his throat, for he understood the reason why. *Such egotism, wanting his image reflected in the Beings!*

The jellyfish gnawed on the tip of one of his tentacles as Allmen rose to his feet, hurried to the stanchions, raised a hand to shade his eyes from the brutal yet shadowy glare, and examined the stark new land and his wife gamboling in its water. She was still clothed in fiery splendor - or had it toned down slightly?

The entire planet seemed to hold its breath as Allmen poised on the deck, deciding. Big-Ego covered his multiple eyes with a mass of medusa-style hair, added another strand to his chewing mouth, and peered through gaps of the tangle. Afraid to look and afraid not to.

'Darling, come!' Divita called, and splashed a desperately playful spray of water towards her husband. Neither of them recognized the amorphous lump lurking in the shallows like a pallid, long-haired slug. There wasn't enough light in the dark sun's rays to find a sparkle or shimmer on his repellant body.

Allmen's heart and mind had been skirmishing almost since his first contact with the jellyfish. Now full-scale war erupted as his built-in desire to love and protect traded punches with the Builder's warning. He could feel the tenderness with which the Builder had spoken, could almost touch his gentle words in the swirling air that felt as comforting as a hug. But overriding all thought and memory and reason was the mind-numbing, all-engulfing panic of separation from Divita, as well as the dangers she might face on the dreadful shore. Their oneness, their union, was at stake. ***I am not complete*** *without her,* he thought, feeling as if he had been sawn in two and was only half alive.

He resolved the jumble of conflicting emotions, the mighty ache of separation and loss, by taking a flying leap off the bow, intending to sprint across the sea's surface to Divita rather than swim. Divita's heart expanded to contain the increase of love mingled with joy, and relief, and gratitude as she saw Allmen choose for her.

He soared through the air like a mighty fireball of light - but the flames extinguished even as the water yawned open beneath his weight.

Unaware that his glory had departed and astonished that the sea hadn't supported him as usual, Allmen rose up in front of Divita in an explosion of noise and white foam.

Divita screamed when she saw him, her voice full of horror as she backed off with her hands over her eyes. And then Allmen screamed, too, as he spotted his wife, and the sounds were like death-rattles. Neither one had ever viewed their spouse stripped bare of glory, and each was more different than they could have imagined.

Divita looked at her body, exposed for the first time, and tears ran down her face - the face Allmen no longer recognized. She tried to hide her nakedness behind her hands and arms, and he did the same, and the shock and reality of what they had done engulfed them like a massive mudslide of death.

Big-Ego discovered in that moment that he actually could laugh, a high-pitched cackle that continued while he danced and twisted and rolled and squirmed in the newly cool water - the rough, pounding water that was rising into liquid mountains with white crests that rolled towards the stark beach with a roar never heard before! Angry waves had never existed. The sky darkened with black clouds that rumbled and crashed, sending shafts of light zigzagging across the sky.

Big-Ego had seen lightning eons before when he was shot off the Island on just such a bolt, but the human Beings who had now become human Doings, never had. It looked and felt like the end of the world, and for them it was: the end of the world as they had known it.

Divita lost her footing as the sea sucked backwards and up into a wall of water that curved above her like a thundering, open-sided tunnel. Allmen grabbed her arm and pulled her to safety up the beach.

'Ouch! You hurt me!' Divita rubbed her bruised arm, her mouth sulky. It was the first good look, after the initial shock, that Allmen had of his wife and it wasn't pleasant. And from the expression in her eyes as she surveyed him, she felt the same way.

'A little "thank you" might be in order. You could have drowned,' he said, annoyed.

'So now you think I can't swim? You are so, so - insufferable!'

'Just the word for you!'

A whiplash smashed across both their backs, leaving raised welts. Stunned into silence after a cry of pain, they looked around to see what had hit them. It was one of Big-Ego's tentacles, stretched taut and slowly receding, and around it, written in charcoal smoke, was the word *strife*. The jellyfish gloated.

'It's all your fault,' Allmen said, turning back to Divita, his voice taut with resentment and accusation.

Divita's features tightened, mirroring her shriveling heart as Allmen's words loosened the last falling petals of her love, leaving it barren as a rose bush facing the onslaught of winter. 'But you –' she stammered, then strengthened. 'You wanted it, too. You know you did. I felt it! That's what pushed me. I did it for you!'

'Oh, how the mighty have fa-a-llen!' sang Big-Ego in an operatic trill.

Glad of an excuse to turn away from Divita's angry, stricken face, Allmen clenched his fists and swung around on the jellyfish - who seemed engorged. A whipping tendril slashed across Allmen's face and another wrapped around his ankle, pulling him off-balance.

Big-Ego rolled and twisted with screeches of uncontrolled laughter. Puffs of dark smoke spelled *Rage* and *Murder* in the air as his tentacles withdrew.

Allmen lay in the sand, humiliated and furious. Huge waves roared ashore and lightning flashed and the crashing clouds thundered. A howling wind hurled stinging sand against his and Divita's shivering bodies, bodies experiencing cold for the first time.

Allmen glanced seaward and jumped to his feet shouting, 'The yacht, the yacht!' But he was too late. A foaming, veined mountain of green water lifted the much-loved hull high and tossed it like a toy onto the beach where it smashed into fragments. And now the rain arrived like a solid curtain of water, slanted in the wind, pelting them with drops that felt hard as flint but were the Builder's soft tears.

Allmen ran to the ruined yacht and, salvaging a piece of the hull, dragged it farther up the beach, out of reach of the raging sea.

'Divita! Come help me here!' he shouted over the roar of the elements. 'The sails could protect us; maybe we can take shelter in the hull.'

As if in a daze, Divita joined him and together they rescued as much as possible and pulled the pieces into a form of protection. They crouched behind it and found refuge from the smarting wind and rain, and waited until the storm passed. Each tried not to look at the other for fear and embarrassment of what they'd see.

Big-Ego's crazy cackle rode the hopeless air of the alien new land.

Chapter 4

The storm's fury refused to abate. As evening approached the temperature plummeted further, and Allmen and Divita were forced into each other's arms for warmth, though they felt like strangers and would have preferred not to touch.

As a gusty, wet dusk settled over the desert a sudden calm descended. The light increased as if it was already dawn and their familiar sun was arriving. Relieved, the two humans raised their heads to look around, and quickly dropped them again as they saw the Builder approaching from beyond the dunes like a tornado on fire as flames of humming glory whirled around him in a roar of windswept sound.

Allmen and Divita now shivered and shook with fear instead of cold.

'Hello, my beloved children, come on out,' called the gentle, deep voice they knew and had loved. But their ears distorted what they heard, so that the Builder sounded to them to be growling in anger.

Eventually Allmen, then Divita, both

wishing they had ten pairs of hands to hide behind, stepped from the protection of the ruined boat, holding bits of wood to cover themselves. The bleak desert land around them was exposed in all its stark emptiness by the Builder's dazzle.

The Builder's eyes moistened afresh as he watched the miserable pair who could not meet his gaze, could not see the light and love there. Their guilt transformed his glorious presence into a threat of punishment.

'My children, my precious children!' The Builder's tears poured like shining rivers over his cheeks. He reached to embrace them but they backed away in terror. He dropped his arms.

'Oh, my children! If only you had believed me, trusted me. In future, in your blindness, peace and joy will come seldom and by your own efforts, and will be a vague shadow of what you knew on the Island where you saw me clearly and we were as one. Indeed, your skin is beginning to blister just from standing in my presence, so great is the heat of your fear of me, who loves you.'

And so it was. Allmen and Divita were

starting to look like boiled lobsters, and all they could hear was non-existent condemnation in the Builder's words.

With sadness etched into his face, the Builder reached up and grabbed a massive white bird as it swooped by, blown in by the storm. It was a sea-dove, something between a huge seagull and a dove, with a thick mantle of feathers. The Builder wrung its neck before it was even aware of being caught, and more tears cascaded down his face.

'My little innocent,' he said to the dead bird. 'My poor little innocent. Never mind, you shall fly again, and not remember this moment. But it will be under a different sky.' He sighed, and repeated the process with another sea-dove. Nimbly his glowing fingers wove their feathers together, fashioning two protective coats. He held them out to Allmen and Divita, who were huddled at a distance.

'Take these cloaks, my darling children. Your minds will perceive them as a covering over your failings; thus the feathers will be like a bridge across an imaginary chasm that your blinded intellects have created between us. For you have decided that I must be angry with you and have consequently withdrawn myself.'

His powerful voice broke on a sob. 'You will explain the loss of my felt presence by saying that my holiness is unable to approach imperfect Doings such as you, and you'll think you need to feathers to hide beneath. But at least while you stand in them you will be able to sense my presence again – a presence which you no longer believe has not, and never will, leave you.'

The Builder sighed, heavily and long, so that the dunes were lit up with his breath and sparks flew from his head as he shook it sadly. He continued speaking, the words reverberating with that sound, as of many voices in tune that yet seemed like just one, which always surrounded him. 'Each time you fail at something, you will feel guilty and ashamed, causing the feather bridge to disintegrate, and you will need to find another bird to sacrifice to your blindness about me, so that you may feel enabled to draw near.

'My children, you will think you are placating me by doing this, but it is to ease your own consciences that you slay the innocent victims that represent your guilt. For guilt brings fear of reprisal; it dims your mind and paints over my face with the colors of darkness.'

Allmen and Divita tried unsuccessfully to understand the meaning of this speech filled with new words; they fiddled with their fingers and their hair and shuffled their feet and wished they were far away, anywhere but standing before the Builder. Though admittedly they did feel much more like their old selves, wrapped in the feather costumes.

The Builder looked at them with all the tender love of the universe glistening in his infinite eyes - and just for a moment, through the feathers, the miserable couple glimpsed it before it was swallowed up in their darkness.

'Nor shall we enjoy the intimacy we once had,' the Builder continued, the words like vinegar in his mouth. 'The feathers will enable you to feel you can approach me, though you will think I am still at a distance. They will provide a few hours or days of respite from your perceived guilt and linked expectation of punishment.' His face contorted with heartbroken pain as he looked into the numberless years of future sacrifices that he didn't need, but which their consciences thought he did. There was no other way for their darkened minds to allow them to cross the gap they now imagined kept them apart.

'There, now I have told you,' he said. 'Oh, how many birds will lose their lives to provide this cover for you!' The Builder's voice was rich with sorrow both for the birds, and for the dark and dreary life that awaited the newly-become Doings.

'Lastly,' he said, 'your food and clothing and shelter from the elements will be achieved by your own hard work and sweat and effort, for you think *you are not* worthy of my provision. You believe you are separated from my love but can earn it back if you try hard enough. You think I am like Big-Ego!'

A thunder-clap startled the two Doings, who looked up fearfully at the swirling clouds, expecting the lash of a tentacle.

The Builder stopped speaking, as if the weight of words was too heavy for his tongue. Then, sighing again, he continued. 'Allmen, you will regain some sense of dignity through the work of your hands; as a result your job will become of primary importance to you and you will strive ever harder to succeed in it, forgetful that all I have is yours already.'

He turned to the female. 'My precious Divita, when you no longer feel my love because of the separation you are convinced exists between us, you will search for that love from your husband, but what he can provide will be a weak substitute for mine. You will be disappointed in him and blame yourself, while his inability to fulfil your expectations will wrap him, too, in a fog of failure. Both of you will believe you are not pretty enough, or strong enough, or any of a million other versions of I-am-notness.'

Now the Builder turned to the jellyfish, who had backed into deeper water to stay cool, but who was nevertheless simpering, only just managing to hold back his victorious, new-found chuckles. The Builder's resonant voice pounded at him like white-hot rays of solid sunlight, tearing into his translucent flesh.

'Big-Ego! Hear me! Your tentacles will become legs, and you'll never swim the depths of the ocean again because of your wicked scheming. You shall be called a scorpion, a creature without any beauty, and none shall be your friend for you will be seen to be a killer to the depths of your blackened heart.'

'But I am now the king of the world!' Big-Ego whined through the pain that began racking his globular body in violent spasms. 'The humans obeyed me instead of you! They betrayed you, and I've usurped them. I'm the king, me, me!'

'Indeed you are, but it is as a scorpion that you shall rule. They have willingly, if un-knowingly, placed themselves under your reign of terror and misery. In that you are correct.' The Builder's next words slammed into Big-Ego with the force of knock-out punches. 'But know this, scorpion, a time will come when one of their descendants snaps off your hooked sting that blinds and deceives; he will restore light and sight and truth to my creation!'

The Builder turned and strode towards the dunes, fresh tears wetting his cheeks. As he left, the darkness skulked back across the land. At the same time Big-Ego experienced an excruciating process of transformation. His translucent, shimmering shape thickened and darkened while he groaned in terror. Something like armor plating grew over the amorphous tissue of his previous body, and a barbed tail formed at one end of him.

The most frightening thing was Big-Ego's size - his new body was as long as Allmen was tall. He was a dreadful spectacle indeed, and looked invincible. A sheen of hatred glinted like icicles in his small eyes as he looked at Allmen and Divita, whom he now blamed for all his woes.

The humans watched the metamorphosis with growing horror. They looked comical in their feathered cloaks, like overgrown white penguins with just their feet and heads peeping out. Their predicament was too awful for them to contemplate.

No more Island. No more Builder. No more glory-glow. No more food plucked from willing plants whenever we felt hungry. No more simply being good, but from now on having to work at doing good in order to try to become good. No more, no more, no more…

'It's all your fault!' Allmen turned on Divita, wagging an accusing finger in front of her nose, the nose he'd only seen shimmering in the glory-glow until recently. He peered closer, and shuddered. Her nostrils sprouted little hairs. And her teeth - he shuddered again: there were remnants of their last meal stuck in their crevices.

Divita's bitter voice lashed back. 'You should have known better! It's your fault, not mine.' They glared at each other, their faces contorted and mean.

Both wondered how they could ever have loved the other.

'Yaah!' yelled Big-Ego, and they swung back to look at him. His huge chest was exposed, bursting with muscles and armor, and his mouth twisted in a nasty grin that said louder than words, 'I'm in charge now! Things are going to change for you!' Behind him a spiked tail curled upwards in a menacing semi-circle. He tested his eight legs, walking towards the Doings with a lumbering gait that grew stronger with each step and left deep prints in the wet sand.

Allmen and Divita had never felt so alone. In a gesture left over from Island days, Allmen put a protective arm around Divita.

Big-Ego's roar of laughter was drowned by

a rush of wind, and suddenly the storm was again upon them, rain lashing and sand flailing their exposed faces. Big-Ego scuttled for cover, and the human Beings, now Doings, waddled behind the wreck of the yacht in their borrowed plumage, trying to retain the joy they'd experienced when the Builder covered them with the innocent feathers, when they had known again his love for them even though they'd brought such calamity upon themselves. But fear had stripped off some of the feathers, and now bitterness and anger ravaged the remainder. They already felt far from the Builder's comforting presence, separated by an expanding chasm that existed only in their distorted minds.

Chapter 5

'Oh, my aching back!' Allmen leaned on his spade, unable to straighten up. His sweating face was weathered, like a three-dimensional map covered in mountains and gullies and dry riverbeds. Each of many, many years of hard toil on the scorched land was reflected there.

He looked around with satisfaction. A section of the desert had come to life under his labor; there were orchards standing proud and bountiful, and fields of wheat sprouting where once only sand had covered the land. Far in the distance the stormy sea raged, its never-ceasing gigantic waves crashing onto the shore. None of his and Divita's descendants could swim, for it was far too rough and dangerous to learn how. The ability to walk on water was a memory he doubted. *Just a dream*, he thought wishfully.

'Lunch time!" Divita's voice carried from the original hut he'd constructed long ago with sunbaked mud bricks. Other shelters had been built as their children grew, and then their children, and then their children. Many, many years, centuries even, had passed. Human Doings were still new on the planet and lived much longer in those days. Roads had needed to be built, and fences. In fact, huts and lanes stretched as far as Allmen could see, on every side.

As he shuffled wearily towards his home, he heard from almost every house the many different sounds of unhappiness. Babies cried, trying to get attention. Children fought in the dust; mothers complained with whining voices; fathers shouted. Husbands criticized the food prepared for them and wives burst into tears or retorted in anger.

Few remembered hearing of the Builder, and they'd forgotten about covering themselves in feathers to feel the peace and joy that came from re-connecting with him. Allmen's memory of those times was vague as a surface mist that sometimes lifted enough to give a momentary, tantalizing glimpse of an erased happiness.

When he reached his hut Divita was standing outside with her hands on her wide hips and a scowl on her wrinkled face.

'Can't you ever be on time? The food's

cold, all my work done for nothing, you selfish, thoughtless man!'

Allmen couldn't remember the sweet and lovely woman he had once known, which was perhaps a good thing because it meant he didn't miss her. He pushed past Divita, nearly knocking her down, and ate his lunch in sullen silence while she muttered in the next room, keeping out of his way.

Divita remembered the old days better than he did. 'I wish he'd look at me once again with eyes full of love,' she mumbled sometimes as she swept the yard. 'Just one more time. Just once.' And she resented her husband for his failings, while pitying herself for all the hardships she endured.

Eventually they both died, and the Island of Being-by-Seeing came to be considered a myth that was hardly ever mentioned. Occasionally a child heard bits of the story of the Island and the Builder, and perhaps something about feathers, and ached to draw close to the vaguely pictured Builder. But catching and killing a sea-dove was not easy or pleasant, and few actually followed through on their longing. By the time they were adults they, too, forgot the stories, or thought they were just that - myths, not truth.

They stopped believing that the Builder existed.

At least, they thought they had stopped believing in him. But sometimes, such as in the cool of a desert sunset when the shadows stretched long and slender from the dunes, and the sky was daubed with the colors of day fading gently into night, there was a flutter of sheer joy in their hearts and for a few moments they dreamed of a different life, one where such feelings weren't transient as the passing twilight. At such times a few wondered where that yearning came from, or, perhaps, of whom it reminded them.

From his palace on the highest hill Big-Ego watched his subjects, and listened, and smiled his twisted smile, and summoned the choir slaves to sing his praises and bow down and chant over and over again how great and powerful and clever he was. He enjoyed mindless repetition, was soothed by its mesmerizing monotony.

The Builder watched too, from the other side of the invisible Wall that was a reflection of the separation between him and them that their minds had created. Its foundation was Big-Ego's wall, which had grown on the same presumption. Now the Wall had grown until it extended from the ocean's surface up over the land of Striving-to-Become in the shape of a dome. Though the Doings believed it separated them from the Builder, he passed through it at will, and often. But his presence went unseen and unnoticed.

Big-Ego disliked the dust and smells of the mud-city stretching across the plain below his mountain palace. The roads were too narrow for his bulk and he was afraid of becoming jammed between houses and being laughed at, though for fear of him the mirth would be hidden behind carefully closed doors. Since there is almost nothing worse than to be the butt of laughter, he stayed inside his palace and ruled from there, and eventually the human Doings forgot about him too, most of the time.

That didn't bother Big-Ego - he sat on his throne and watched and listened and whenever he saw an opportunity, one of Big-Ego's specialized whips would snake out and raise a welt on the Doing's back or shoulders, welts that left scars. Snap, crack, and the Doing would feel worse than ever.

Each wound carried embedded in it a penetrating sense of failure. The lash penetrated through their skin, branding into their heart and mind Big-Ego's snarling, personalized litany of 'you are nots': *You are nothing; you're a failure and you'll never be anything else; you are not worthy; you are not lovable; you are not good enough; or beautiful enough; or thin enough; or successful enough; you'll never get it right, this is the millionth time you've tried, give up, believe me and know you are not, are not, are not anything at all.*

The Doings no longer realized that their pain and accompanying low self-esteem was caused by the scorpion's whips, or by his hooked tail.

They hid their wounds under clothing so others wouldn't notice, and listened to the scorpion's whispers and believed them, which freed the poison to flow freely. They kept adding more clothes to hide the seeping bleeding of every fresh laceration, or when the old ones were opened by a new accusation as to what or who they were not…

They became protective of their wounds, secretive, and fearful of them being discovered. So they pretended to everyone that they were better than they thought they were, which caused a rising stress factor to take up residence inside them, and subsequently a disintegration of personal relationships. Their blindness to the Builder's character deepened with their shame, but their eyes were so accustomed to it they no longer knew that they lived in darkness; and the Wall they thought separated them from the Builder appeared thicker all the time, ever more insurmountable.

Big-Ego also taught them that every scar would be counted when they died and if they had too many, they might not make it into the place in the sky, or to the fabled Island, or wherever it was they thought good people went to.

Worst of all, no one knew how many scars were 'too many.' Of course, everybody wanted to be good enough to move to somewhere pleasant when they died, and so they kept trying and trying to earn points by good behavior, which they believed was the way to raise their scores. But they found that the harder they tried, the more they failed. The stuff they weren't supposed to do became the stuff they did.

'Oh, oh,' some of the Doings would mutter after shouting a mean word at a son or daughter who was late for dinner, or had torn clothing while climbing a tree. 'Oh, oh, why can't I be nicer? Surely there is a way for me to become a better person? Surely?' From somewhere deep inside them there was a sense of hope that they could change, and indeed, sometimes they did – for a while. But keeping doing everything right all the time proved impossible, and soon the anger was back in their voices, and they wondered why they had ever thought they could be different.

Because of the perceived Wall of Separation, there was no way the Doings could hear the Builder's voice speaking to their hearts that he loved them for who they were, whether they failed or succeeded, and that his love had nothing whatsoever to do with their behavior. He simply loved them.

He watched as the days passed into years

and then centuries, and waited for the time to ripen to fullness, when he could initiate his rescue plan.

Occasionally a Doing found him- or herself pondering about where this ever-returning passion to be a better Doing originated. Their thoughts would turn to vague snippets once heard about a wonderful Builder, and for a few moments a flickering little flame would penetrate the great darkness in which they lived. And then it would sputter out. *If there is a Builder*, they thought, *he'll be disappointed in me. **I am not** good enough for him. How could I ever hope to live up to his expectations, his standards of perfection? He surely could never love me.*

Eventually, through the unending hopelessness caused by their belief in I-am-notness, fibs escalated into lies; anger became rage; gossip and slander, which killed people's characters, became murder of their bodies. The Builder saw that the Doings had lost all sense of direction. Deep down they wanted desperately to feel closer to him, but they didn't know where to begin, or who he was, or more to point, *how* he was, how good, kind, loving, powerful, gentle. It was time to step back into the situation with some guidelines.

Chapter 6

One fresh cloudless morning there was an earsplitting drum roll of thunder over the land of Striving-to-Become. The huts and fields still sparkled with the previous night's dew, and only a few early risers had set off to work. The noise was loud enough to waken those still asleep, and stop the others at whatever they were busy with. Everyone ran outside and looked up at the sky, and began shouting or screaming or wailing or crying because of what they saw there.

It seemed as if a mighty mountain floated above the town, and the Doings were certain it was about to drop and squash them all. How could anything so heavy stay up in the air?

A child was the first to notice movement on the suspended land mass. 'Look,' he shouted, pointing, 'look, humans!'

Everyone gaped and squinted and stared, and sure enough soon all could see movement at the base of the peak where a golden beach stretched in languid loveliness, edged by palms and jungle foliage swaying in an ever-present light breeze.

'Aah!' There was a collective gasp as what seemed to be two walking, glowing torches moved onto the sand into plain view.

The Builder had crossed the time-line and from the far past, brought the Island of Being-by-Seeing to the sky above the land of Striving-to-Become, suspending it there in all its gentle loveliness.

For a week the people watched Allmen and Divita (whom they didn't recognize in their glory-glow) as they lived in an abandonment of conscious, accepting love nourished by the living air, as they spoke kindly to each other, played together, and fellowshipped with the Builder in laughter and happiness. For a week the Doings were exposed to a view of life as it was meant to be lived, as they had never experienced or imagined it could be.

It was a life of *being* instead of *trying to become* powered by individual lists of *I am nots*. *Being* good, kind, gentle, loving, patient, joyful, peaceful, humble and self-controlled because they already were all those things simply because they were created so in the Builder's image and they could hear the Builder's voice guiding them and chatting with them from inside. The Doings were lost in the darkness that blinded their eyes to who the Builder was and how much he loved them - from inside them.

The Island hung below Big-Ego's palace and blocked his view and dulled his hearing, and separated him from the Doings for the full week.

And then the Island began to fade and diminish until the sky was once again empty except for the faded, blazing sun and a few blank, fluffy clouds. The Doings sobbed as they watched the vision disappear.

There was another crash of thunder from the clear blue, and suddenly the Wall appeared, now as solid and visible as the Island had been. More thunder, and then a bolt of lightning lit the firmament much brighter than the dull sun.

'Aahh!!!' The Doings cried out as a huge glory-covered hand grabbed the lightning and, holding it like a pencil, began to write, burning words into the Wall and trailing golden light-dust.

The Doings had never experienced such brightness. They squinted at the forming words while shielding their eyes.

Sentences formed, ten of them. They spelled out what made the Island different, while also showing what the Builder was like. For example, because he was full of love he would never steal possessions, or a wife or husband, from a neighbor or even a stranger, because his love extended to everybody.

The Sentences were also meant to explain that by acting unlovingly and going against the Sentences, the Doings would be acting against their own nature, which was created exactly like the Builder's - so they would be wounding themselves as well as others. The Sentences were guidelines to healthy living for the floundering Doings.

The lightning-rod pencil finished writing. The Builder tossed it into the vibrant air and waited as the Doings read the Sentences. When they finished, a huge shout rose up from them, so loud it shook the walls of Big-Ego's palace and filled him with terror.

'Yes!' they cried. 'Yes! We will *do* all that you have written, oh Builder. We will, yes, we will!'

'No, you won't,' the Builder whispered,

surveying them sadly. 'You won't be able to, for you have been infected by Big-Ego's darkness and now live in his blindness. But the Sentences will give you a starting place, a pointer towards a brighter life. They will remove one or two of the fuzzy lenses through which you view me.' He wiped a tear and continued under his breath. 'The Sentences reflect my goodness and love and are meant to show you what I am like.'

All of this was said too quietly for the Doings to hear. The Builder's glowing face filled with joy, then saddened. This was only a beginning, the vaguest glimpse of who he was. It would take much, much more to penetrate their darkness, to bring light to the eyes that could no longer see him inside them. This was indeed his greatest sorrow, to be living in them, unknown and unacknowledged while they remained ignorant of his loving and accepting presence.

But as the Builder looked at the Doings, his smile returned. They were worth it. He loved them. Even though they were busy doing mean and hurtful things to each other in their daily blindness about him, he loved them as parents love their children even though they might be naughty or disobedient. He loved them that way, but infinitely more than even the best parent ever could.

When the timing was finally right he would invade their darkness and rescue them. It was all in the timing.

The Sentences remained burnt into the Wall, which, however, had become invisible again. So the words seemed to be written on the sky, visible for the Doings to see all the time, day and night.

Big-Ego sat in his palace, ruminating over what he'd heard about the past week, and about the writing in the sky.

'Aha!' he thought. 'The Builder is trying to change the Doings. But it's too late; they're all infected with my virus of Striving-to-Become. And I'll show him, I'll use those Sentences *against* the Doings. I'll twist all those "good-things-to-be" Sentences into "more-things-to-do!' He chuckled, and beat his chest, and called the choir to come again and sing about how clever he was – way cleverer than the Builder.

Chapter 7

The Doings read the Sentences day after day, and tried hard to put the good things into practice, but they always failed. And each time they failed, the whip slashed their backs and shoulders. They had more scars than ever, many more than before the Sentences were written. One evening they called a meeting around the central fire in the main square.

'What shall we do?' they cried. And some of the braver ones admitted, 'We are covered in scars from all our failures!'

An old man, wrinkled and bent, raised his walking stick in the air and when everyone was silent, began to speak.

'I remember when I was young,' he said, 'I heard a story about feathers. If we killed sea-doves and covered ourselves with their feathers, we'd be able to come closer to the Builder.'

There was an uproar. 'Can this be true?' everyone shouted. Some, just a few, remembered having heard such a story. The excitement was immense. The Doings jumped and danced. They decided to choose a group of men to be responsible for catching and killing the sea-doves and handing out the feathers. They named these men the Special Doings.

Sure enough, the feathers from the slaughtered, innocent sea-doves worked. The scars and their aches disappeared until the next time. a Sentence was broken. The Doings would draw closer to the Builder who, though he was heartbroken about the sea-doves, knew there was no other way to communicate again with his creations. Using dreams, he explained to the Special Doings how to cause the sea-doves the least pain; meanwhile he longed for the day when the Doings would recognize his love and toss away the sacrificial practice - when they realized it wasn't the Builder but rather their own darkness that convinced them of imaginary unworthiness; of being undeserving of the Builder's love - not realizing it was unconditional. This indeed was beyond their understanding.

Imbedded in this practice of killing an innocent on behalf of the guilty was a hint of the cosmic-affecting murder that they would commit in the future.

And so, though hope glowed in the hearts

of the Doings as they experienced the peace of feeling forgiven for all their faults whenever they were covered with the feathers, their awful blindness prevented them from seeing that the longed-for forgiveness was freely available, permanently and without cost, and kept them ignorant of his infinitely loving presence inside them.

Instead, they always, always felt as if they didn't measure up, as if they weren't good enough to be loved by the Builder. Their ears were tuned in to the scorpion's wavelength, which broadcast only his list of *you-are-nots.*

Nevertheless, for a little while things improved enough to worry Big-Ego. He re-doubled his efforts to twist the Sentences, which were meant to be guiding lights, into stones that tripped the Doings up. Soon each quality of life that had been normal on the Island became a burden to the Doings, who failed miserably as they tried and tried to live like Allmen and Divita - free, happy, and full of fun.

Since they didn't know and couldn't believe that the Builder inhabited them, they didn't know how precious they actually were, and it was easy to believe Big-Ego's lies of I-am-notness, and consequently to do bad rather than good things. For, unfortunately, they acted out their lives from their distorted heart-beliefs about themselves, or from trying to disguise their failures in order to be acceptable.

Hundreds of years passed. The scars came and went, came and went, as Big-Ego pointed out the Doings' offences and then they received the Builder's forgiveness when they approached him in their innocent-feather cloaks. But their clouded self-image prevented the Doings from being good for long, and they became worn out with trying and failing and trying again.

Incredibly, somewhere in their depths, there remained a tiny glow of hope glimmering in their darkness, hope that somehow, someway, some day, things would change; that the Builder would step in and restore the Island's way of being. The hope whispered a promise into their souls that life wasn't meant to be so tough, that their brokenness was temporary, that something wonderful and good and beautiful waited around some corner or down some path.

Finally the Builder saw that the Doings were, at last, ready for his awesome rescue plan. One human Being, Allmen, had blinded all Beings, ushering in Big-Ego's darkness and turning the Beings into Doings when he, as their representative, mistrusted the Builder and chose instead to believe the lie of a deceiving jellyfish.

As a Being, Allmen had been free of Big-Ego's infection of blindness to the Builder's love and presence, so another human Being was entitled arrive on the scene, equally uninfected, to open the Doings' mental eyes with the glory of the Builder's light. And what a Being he would be! – for the Builder himself was about to take on a Doing body in all its weakness, and become one of them.

On a velvet, starry night in winter, shockwaves surged through the cosmos that the Builder had created, as, motivated by his magnificent love, he put aside his glory-glow and all his vast powers and was born miraculously into the murky land of Striving-to-Become - as a baby Doing named Word-Withus.

Word-Withus grew up like all the other Doing boys - except that, because he wasn't infected with Big-Ego's blindness he never once succumbed to the temptation of doing a single loveless act, or believed the 'I-am-nots' that Big-Ego broadcast endlessly.

By the time he was a teenager he had worked out who he was, and what his purpose was.

Big-Ego had been sniffing the air since Word-Withus's birth, smelling something clean and fresh and light-filled that brought back memories of the Island. He sent slaves to search for the source of the aroma, but somehow they never found Word-Withus. Big-Ego decided he was growing old and that was why he kept getting whiffs of the Island. *Or maybe,* he thought one day when the aroma was strong, *maybe the ceaseless storm that pushes up those enormous, wild waves that cover the ocean, is calming, allowing the Island scent to float over the waters?*

Big-Ego was now too well-fed to move much, but he ordered a gang of slaves to carry him to the beach so that he could investigate. Several collapsed along the way. Big-Ego ordered them rolled into ditch beside the road, to die in the heat.

The litter carrying the lounging eight-legged monster stopped at the head of the beach, from where he examined the scene for several minutes.

Hmm, he thought. *The waves are every bit as big as they were, and as always, anyone who manages to swim past the first ones will bump into the invisible Wall with its very visible writing.*

'Home!' he ordered with a clack of his waving claws. The slaves sweated and gasped and struggled back up the hill under their enormous, bad-tempered load.

One morning soon afterwards Big-Ego awoke, absolutely certain that he was back on the Island. The palace, including his bedroom, was filled with fresh, healthy air blowing in from outside and carrying with it a voice that the scorpion recognized - the Builder's voice.

'Help!' Big-Ego shouted. 'Slaves, protect me! Help!'

Nobody came. He cringed in his bed and waited for the Builder to arrive.

Nothing happened. The voice continued

speaking, the fresh scent wafted through the palace on a light breeze. Finally Big-Ego struggled out of bed and, looking more like a slug than a scorpion, waddled to the window.

Below him a huge crowd, including most of his slaves, milled around the town square. They were listening, spellbound, to a young man clarifying some points of the Sentences.

Big-Ego frowned. The young Doing had the Builder's voice! Yet otherwise he was quite dissimilar - for starters, there was no glow. Surprisingly, Big-Ego found himself liking what the Doing was saying, for he was adding to the Sentences, making them even more difficult to 'do'. He seemed to be showing the Doings clearly that the Sentences were even more difficult than they had seemed.

'Yes, oh yes!' Big-Ego agreed, and applauded with several forelegs and a broad grin. "Make them harder, yes!"

Nevertheless, it was strange how fresh the air smelled.

In his blindness the scorpion could not see that the Sentences were a reflection of the Builder's character, which Word-Withus was defining even more clearly.

The Doings were in the same place of darkness as Big-Ego, and were distraught.

Chapter 8

Word-Withus looked up at the palace walls from his position in the square, sensing that that was where the increased stench of disease and death was coming from.

Ah, he thought, frowning, *of course.* For a moment a picture flashed across his mind, of Big-Ego with another name, another shape, singing magnificently in the days before he'd been consumed by I-am-not envy over the Builder's galactic authority, and had yearned for that place of lordship himself. And he wanted to earn the glory-glow by his own efforts so that he could be self-righteous instead of Builder-righteous.

Meanwhile, the Doings were distraught by Word-Withus's teachings. How could they ever hope to obey these even tougher Sentences? He was telling them that being angry with someone was a bad as hitting them with a fist!

Word-Withus smiled at them while his heart thumped with his huge love. Right now they couldn't grasp his point, that the Sentences reflected the Builder - they showed how perfectly loving he was, how perfectly good in every way.

'Don't worry, my dear friends,' Word-Withus said. 'The Builder will make a way.' When he finished teaching, he touched all the sick Doings and made them well, and created food out of the cleansed air around him and fed them, and told them about how much the Builder loved them, and other wonderful things they hadn't known about him.

At first, for fear of the scorpion, the Doings only whispered about the astonishing miracles and healings that occurred at Word-Withus's hands. Later, the talk couldn't be contained to corners; it became the conversation of the land.

Big-Ego was no longer pleased with what Word-Withus said, but with his slaves still missing there was no way to stop him. He went back to bed with his hooked tail whipping about uncontrollably, smashing lamps and porcelain ornaments, and covered his ears with a gold-embroidered pillow.

Soon the Doings were discussing nothing but Word-Withus and his miracles, and his assurances that the Builder loved them and hadn't forgotten them. While they listened they were filled with excitement, but the darkness over their minds prevented the news from rooting in their hearts. Still the talk continued. Could Word-Withus be the one they'd been waiting for, the one who'd free them and restore Island life to them?

Day by day Word-Withus removed layers of lenses through which the Doings saw the Builder. He explained that the Sentences weren't written to make life tougher, but to reflect the loving nature of the Builder who would never envy or murder or cheat because of the love at his core that overflowed to all creation.

Huge crowds followed him. Even children wanted to listen to him because he taught with stories that they could understand. Every sick Doing he touched became well again - even dead ones were made alive! The murmur of hope mushroomed louder across the land – was Word-Withus the one who would defeat the scorpion?

It was a time of rejoicing - except for Big-Ego. The more the Doings listened to Word-Withus, the more Big-Ego's hatred increased.

The scorpion woke up scheming of ways to stop the healings and silence the good words about the Builder's nature; he passed the days devising plots and plans, and in his silken, down-filled bed at night there was still nothing else on his mind.

'I'll arrest him,' he growled from his embroidered cushions – and then realized Word-Withus would heal the prisoners locked up with him and tell them of the Builder and his love for them. No, jail wasn't the answer. Beating Word-Withus up would madden the Doings, who venerated him, so that also wouldn't help matters. Kidnapping him and dropping him off in the middle of the desert might work, but then again Word-Withus might find his way home.

There is only one option. Word-Withus must die.

Big-Ego put all his brainpower to work on planning how to make it happen without himself seeming to be involved, and eventually an idea formed for Word-Withus to be outwitted, shown to be a charlatan, and sentenced to death.

One bright morning - the air around Word-

Withus always seemed to glow as if it was newly washed and hung out to dry - Word-Withus was again telling a group of Doings in the town square about the Builder's love. He sighed as he spoke the saddest words ever to pass his lips, words that, if understood, would explain everything about the Doings' situation, about him and about his mission. 'The problem,' he said distinctly, 'is that no Doing, not a single one but me, knows the Builder.'

Up in the palace Big-Ego heard Word-Withus's words and responded with thunderous rage. He pushed himself off the silk cushions that supported his ungainly body. 'Slaves!' he yelled. 'Bring my litter!' It was time for a confrontation.

Meanwhile, a commotion at the edge of the square interrupted the gathering.

'Move! Out of our way!' The Special Doings Police shoved through the crush, knocking an old woman over and breaking her walking stick as they trampled it underfoot. Dragged between them was a young girl of ten or twelve, dressed in rags. Her bony arms were purpling with rising bruises from the cruel grips of the burly SDP, and her fearful, dirty face was streaked with tears.

'Caught stealing, she was. Caught red-handed. And not for the first time! I ought to break her rotten arms, then see if she'd be able to help herself to unpaid fruit from the vendor!' The speaker, the biggest of the policemen, was pumped with indignation. He hurled the girl forward, sending her sprawling on the ground at Word-Withus's feet. She buried her tangled head of hair in her arms and tried to choke her sobs.

'See here, Word-Withus,' said the muscled officer, 'you keep talking all this forgiveness and love goop, but the Sentences say that a thief's gotta be stoned to death. And them Sentences was written by the Builder hisself, right? So now whatcha gonna do, hey?!'

Just out of sight around a corner, a group of Special Doings listened with smirks pasted across their faces. 'Let's see him get out of *this,*' one of them whispered, nudging another in his ribs.

They had arranged the setup on orders from the palace, and had followed a known thief until they caught her committing a crime.

Word-Withus leaned over and ruffled the

girl's matted hair. It began to gleam like burnished gold, as if a brighter sun had come out from behind a cloud in the cloudless sky.

Somebody in the crowd broke the silence with a gasp. 'Look, the bruises - they've disappeared!' The girl did not raise her head.

The old woman who had been knocked down felt for her broken stick. She couldn't bear the sight of the child alone on the ground. She took the biggest half of the stick and used it to hobble forward on her knees, dragging her lame leg behind, until she was beside the waif. She glared up protectively and her eyes shouted soundlessly, *Don't even try to touch her, you big oafs.* Fortunately for her she didn't voice her thoughts out loud.

The old woman saw the corners of Word-Withus's mouth twitch ever so slightly, almost as if he'd heard her thought… and then the full force of the love in Word-Withus's gaze caught her, entered her, tugged at her heart, tingled through her body - tingled through her paralyzed leg! How could that be when there was no feeling possible? Her anger dissipated like boiling bubbles of soup when the heat is turned off. She didn't need to stand up to prove it, she knew: she was healed.

'Well?' said the policeman, his voice almost a growl; he was unaware that the world had tilted for what, in his opinion, was one worthless old person. 'What's it gonna be, huh?'

Word-Withus's compelling gaze focused on the pack of SD Police, lingering on each one. Unnerved, their accusing stares wavered.

A few of the Doings in the gathering felt a little flame of courage ignite inside, enough to permit their hearts to reach towards a sort of hopeless hope. But then they looked from Word-Withus to the Special Doings and thought, *No, the Special Doings are so righteous and holy and they follow all the Sentences, we should listen to them, not Word-Withus.* And the little flame fizzled.

The Special Doings had convinced themselves and the Doings that they, the SDs, were doing just fine at obeying the Sentences (although they overlooked the first one, which spoke about loving the Builder and all the Doings...).

Word-Withus turned back to the Special Doings Police, the SDP, who were glowering at him, the girl and the old woman. He was in a tricky position. According to the Law of Sentences, thieves were to be stoned to death. And everyone knew that the Builder's lightning bolt had written the Sentences.

'You've brought this girl to me because you caught her stealing, and that means she must die. Is that correct?' Though Word-Withus's voice was low, it carried. The people in the square shuffled nervously, sensing an approaching showdown.

Gruff SDP voices muttered agreement. Around the dusty corner the Special Doings huddled together, almost salivating in their self-righteousness as they wondered how the upstart was going to extricate himself from this carefully organized situation - for they had arranged for the SDP to stalk the girl and catch her in the act.

'We've got him this time, for sure,' whispered one, covering his mouth with his hand to hide a giggle.

A robed Special Doing beside him raised an eyebrow. He'd been around when Word-Withus extricated himself from other difficult situations; he wasn't quite as sure of the outcome as his companion.

In the background an older Special Doing watched with a puzzled expression, and, unlike the others of his brotherhood, hoped against his good sense that this strange and gentle young man would come up with a plan. But what? How could he extricate himself from this conundrum? The SD laws were based on the Sentences, which were written by the Builder. How then could Word-Withus, who said he knew the Builder, go against the Builder, the SDs, the SDP, their Law?

The crowd waited, increasingly tense.

'Hmm', murmured Word-Withus. 'Well, then, why not let the perfect Doing who has never once disobeyed any of the Sentences be the one to pick up and throw the first stone at this little girl. Doesn't that sound fair?'

While he spoke he stretched his arm and made twirling movements in the air with his index finger. The Doings glanced at one another questioningly. It almost looked as if he were writing. 'His finger,' they whispered, jostling each other, 'is it glowing like a lightning bolt, or is that an illusion of the morning sun's reflected light?' Whatever, the angle of his letters meant they were only legible to the Special Doings and the SDP.

After the police read the words glowing in the crisp air, one by one, eyes down, they slunk away. When they turned the corner, there were no longer any Special Doings waiting there.

The crowd of Doings let out their breaths in a great, combined sigh of relief. But how they longed to know what the writing had said!

Word-Withus touched the girl, who recoiled in fear. He squatted beside her so that she could see the love shining from his face. 'Child,' he said, 'look around and tell me, where are your accusers?'

One quick, nervous glance showed her that the SDP had left. She turned back to Word-Withus and almost forgot to answer him as they locked gazes again and she was swept into the wells of compassion she found in his eyes.

'There is no one left, sir.'

Word-Withus's face lit up even more as he grinned. 'Well child, I don't find you guilty either. And now, knowing you're forgiven, and remembering the love I have for you, do you think you'll ever want to steal again?'

'Oh sir, no! Never. All the hurt and anger is gone – I've seen your love and it has changed me! Thank you sir. Thank you!' She turned to the old woman, intending to help her up, but there was no need - for the old lady was standing straight and tall on two well legs.

'I offer you my home if you need it, little one,' said the woman, and now, finally, the girl's pinched face was transformed by a wide smile.

As they left together after hugging Word-Withus, Big-Ego's litter rounded the opposite corner of the square, borne on the sweating shoulders of an army of slaves.

But Word-Withus was no longer there. He had simply - gone.

The Special Doings felt the same way about Word-Withus as the scorpion did. They hated him with intense ferocity. Like Big-Ego, they had become inflated with self-importance. They thought that being part of the Special brigade meant they were more important than other Doings. They made themselves rich by cheating the Doings out of their hard-earned wages, charging inflated prices for the sea-dove feathers so that the Doings were forced into debt in order to buy forgiveness, or were even prevented from affording it.

Until Word-Withus came along, the Special Doings were well-satisfied with life in the Land of Striving-to-Become.

They called a secret meeting to discuss him, gathering in a room with thick walls, no windows, and one heavy wooden door which they closed and bolted after everyone arrived. Burning torches attached to the stone walls cast flickering shadows over the hooded figures.

'Who does Word-Withus think he is?' snarled a Special Doing. 'He told me that my high prices were stopping some Doings from affording feathers, and so it was my fault that they couldn't get the Builder's forgiveness, and he knocked my day's profit onto the floor!'

'He told me that being rich wasn't enough, I should be kind and gentle too!' said another, his voice bristling with anger.

Another Special Doing stood up. 'I asked him who he thought he was, and he answered, "Who do you think I am?" So I said, "You act like you're the Builder." And then he looked at me weirdly and said, "You said it!" Now what's that supposed to mean, huh?'

'Seems to me this guy thinks he's as good as the Builder,' said the first speaker. 'I say let's have it knocked out of him. After all, *we're* the Special Doings, not him!'

'Yeah, the Builder chose *us* to teach the Doings all the things they must do to please him,' said someone else, rising and pacing around the room, quite unaware of the lie he had just perpetrated.

'Yes!' everyone shouted. 'And let's not forget, if we didn't kill the sea-doves and make the feather cloaks, the Doings would all be goners. There's no forgiveness and right-standing without the covering feathers from innocent sacrificed birds, that's for sure.'

'So what's to be done?' asked their chief, the Big Deal Special Doing.

After much discussion they decided to hire a gang of thugs to corner Word-Withus in a dark alley and beat him to a pulp.

'Make sure they break a few bones, y'know, keep him out of our way for a while,' said the Big Deal.

A breath of air flickered the torch flames. None of the Special Doings wondered how a breeze could get into the closed, windowless room.

Chapter 9

Word-Withus lay on his back under star shine bright as crystal droplets, on a hillside not far from Doings Town and Big-Ego's palace, and chatted with the Builder. Word-Withus, of course, was the Builder, but there's more to it than that. He was the Builder - but not all the Builder. Until Word-Withus's arrival nobody had understood (though some scholars had quietly surmised) that the Builder was a union of three persons who loved each other so perfectly that they were inseparably one, yet remained distinct and separate entities who retained their individuality within the 'oneness.'

Well, Word-Withus Builder was part of Papa Builder and Papa was part of Word-Withus, and that's about as close an explanation as there is; their third part was Tender Storm. She was the shy one of the three, but also, perhaps, the most powerful, absorbing the holy beauty of the others and reflecting it back to them, hugging them in her love-light. And she was invisible, as the wind is.

From their relationship of mutual indwelling love whose depth is beyond comprehension, originates and flows all that is good and beautiful in the universe.

Word-Withus Builder shifted his shoulders into a more comfortable position on the sandy ground while Tender Storm Builder told him of the Special Doings' plans - for Tender Storm had been the gentle breeze at the secret meeting, which nobody noticed. Papa, knowing everything, was already aware.

'The reason I became a Doing was to penetrate their blind mis-understanding of us, which is only possible through entering into and plumbing the deepest depths of their depravity,' Word-Withus said softly. 'There is no other way to reach right into their darkness and open the eyes of their hearts. We know how rough that's going to be, so why are you worried about a little thing like me being attacked?'

'Because it's not yet time,' said Tender Storm Builder. 'You will suffer one day, but not yet. I suggest taking a vacation, staying out of sight for a while.'

Word-Withus smiled slowly, a twinkle dancing in his eyes. 'No, Storm, I'm not going to hide. If you don't want me beaten up, you'd better stay close by, cover me in your invisibility when I need it.'

Tender Storm laughed back that she never left him anyway, but then continued more seriously. 'You may not use your enormous power while you're a Doing, but you can use mine in and through you. As the Doings could if they only knew me. So, yes, let's do it that way.' She bounced a ball of love-light at Word-Withus and Papa, and disappeared.

Word-Withus rested on the hillside for another hour, chatting with Papa Builder. As dawn arrived in glowing shades of pastel, Papa Builder leaned forward and pulled his son close in a bear hug. He bent to kiss his head before speaking.

'You know, my son, what hurts the most? More than the distorted view of me they believe in, more even than the separation they are convinced exists between them and us, and the Wall they imagine is real? The most devastating misconception of all is that they will blame me when you die, will say I required you to sacrifice yourself to appease the anger their darkened minds think I hold against them.'

Word-Withus changed position and wrapped his arms around Papa. 'Never mind,' he murmured, 'let's focus on the joy, theirs and ours, when they finally see and know the truth.'

Soon afterwards Word-Withus set off down the hill to Doings Town, where a crowd already waited, filled with anxious questions.

'Sir, Mr. Word-Withus, sir,' they called, jostling to get near him. One young man made it to the front, his brown eyes sincere, pleading. 'Sir, yesterday you forgave the thief - sir, what if she steals again, would you forgive her again?'

'I would indeed,' Word-Withus said with a chuckle.

'How many times sir? What if she stole three times?'

'Then she'd be forgiven three times.'

'How many times should I forgive someone, altogether, sir?'

'Seven times,' Word-Withus said. The crowd gasped.

'Oh. Oh dear.' The intense face before Word-Withus crumpled, then brightened as its owner rose to the challenge. 'Okay sir, I'll try. Even seven times.' The crowd murmured approval and the young man's shoulders straightened - proudly.

Word-Withus sighed. They were missing the point, again. The Builder would forgive as many times as was needed. 'Actually, young man - Kenny, isn't it? - I think it's more like seventy times seven,' he said, and strode on down the dusty street while the crowd tried to make sense of what they'd just heard.

As Kenny wondered how Word-Withus knew his name, and tried to work out how much seventy times seven added up to, a gust of air blew a lock of hair across his brow as if teasing him; he absent-mindedly pushed it back.

That afternoon Word-Withus returned to the base of the hillside where he'd spent the night, again followed by a large crowd. This time he taught them about money, for their finances were carefully watched over by the Special Doings, who insisted that they pay at least a tenth of their earnings to them, and who then added many more financial burdens above that. They SDs taught the Doings to sow money 'seeds' in order to reap money harvests, intimating that the Builder was like a banker in the sky who could not help them financially unless they first gave him some of their money to work with. So the Builder was no longer seen as a Papa who provided for his precious Doing children because he loved them, but was pictured instead as a business investor.

Word-Withus waited for the Doings to get comfortable before he taught. He stretched out his hand and a little robin alighted there, gazing into his face with total trust. Other birds flew over the crowd as if fascinated by the teacher.

"Look at those birds,' Word-Withus began. He took a breath before continuing, knowing that what he said next was going to provoke the Special Doings and their police force. 'Look and see how the Builder provides for them. They don't give tenths, or sow money, or worry about harvesting dividends - yet the Builder looks after them. And my dear Doings, you are worth far more to the Builder than the birds are.'

The Doings murmured in surprise.

'He will always provide for you,' Word-Withus continued, 'and he'll do so because he loves you. It's as simple as that, if you could but believe it. Truly, it's not about works but about worth - your worth!'

'Rubbish!' cried a voice from the back. 'Nonsense! This is treason against the Builder! Word-Withus is teaching you not to tithe!' It was the Big Deal Special Doing himself, infuriated beyond self-control. His face was puffed red with anger and he pounded his fist as if it was a hammer and he wished Word-Withus was a nail.

Word-Withus longed to speak more, to explain that generosity from a heart full of love and gratitude was what the Builder had in mind, rather than a command that was obeyed for the selfish result of increase, or to placate him. He shuddered, wishing to talk about stingy Doings who hoarded all their gains, and to explain that the Builder wanted rather for them to have fun and enjoy the fruits of their hard work, literally and financially.

But the crowd's mood had changed. The

people were incensed, snorting objections like angry bulls. Word-Withus rose. It was pointless to continue in this atmosphere.

He moved into the throng, heading home. But this time no gap opened amongst the Doings. Instead Word-Withus felt a thump on his shoulder. He stumbled, saw another arm raised against him as the crowd jostled him - and then he was looking down at them from the hilltop, watching them turn in surprised circles, searching for him.

'Thanks, Storm,' he said, and felt a breath move across his brow.

Word-Withus and Tender Storm spent the rest of the day together, discussing ways to explain to the Doings what the Builder was really like. The Sentences had been misinterpreted until the all-loving Builder was now thought to be a scary old man in the sky holding a big stick, waiting to cane them for the slightest misdemeanor. In fact, that was Big-Ego's role, but he'd disguised his part well.

As dusk fell, Word-Withus and Tender Storm heard a scrabbling and huffing and patter of dislodged pebbles. Tender Storm floated over the pathway leading to the hill's crown, and Word-Withus felt her smile.

Chapter 10

Soon a Special Doing's turban came into view perched precariously above a red face off which rivulets of perspiration dripped onto a thick rolled collar. Word-Withus rose to lend him a hand up the final section of the steep slope.

'Welcome,' Word-Withus said, seating himself again on the rock that had served as a chair all afternoon, and indicating another for the elderly SD.

'Thought I'd find you here, youngster, though how you managed it I don't know.' The older man wiped his forehead and then the rest of his face with a square of cloth. 'I wanted to help you, down there. Couldn't get through in time. I see I needn't have worried.'

'I knew your good intention. And, my thanks to you. May I call you Sincere Heart, or would you prefer Sir?'

The Special Doing forgot his tiredness. 'How... how do you know my name?' It was he who had stood in the background, hoping against hope, when the young thief had been brought to Word-Withus.

'That's not the question you came here to ask me, I think.' Word-Withus's eyes twinkled, but there was gravity there too. He gestured again for the Special Doing to take a seat, which he did with a grunt.

'Indeed, I have many questions, and that's not one of them, you're right. My problem is this: who are you? You perform miracles - but by who's power? Only the Builder can do such things, but I don't see the Builder before me. I see a young upstart and I want to know what's going on, that's what I want to know, seeing as you asked!'

Word-Withus's chuckle turned to full-boiled laughter. Sincere Heart was both relieved, for he hadn't intended to be quite so uppity, and annoyed, for his questions had been serious. He was grateful for a light breeze cooling his sweaty skin.

Word-Withus wiped his laughter-wet cheeks and answered. 'You know, my friend, if the Builder was standing here before you, you wouldn't recognize him because you need spiritual eyes to understand and see him and the things of his kingdom. The only way to get those eyes working is to breathe the Builder's pure breath that expels darkness and deceit.' The leaves above their heads rustled.

Sincere Heart looked up quizzically and nodded his turban, though he didn't really understand.

'Unfortunately, it isn't possible for you, or any Doing, to breathe that way because you're all infected with the scorpion's foul breath of death. It's that polluted breath that built the original wall. Dear friend, when the Wall tumbles down, all will breathe in the Builder's life-giving breath. They may not know it, but the very air will change back to Island air.'

The Special Doing leaned forward. 'Show me how to breathe his breath and I'll break down the Wall!' he said, his old eyes bright.

'Ah, there's the problem. You cannot. You've been trying since Allmen's day.'

Sincere Heart raised his palms. 'There is no hope then. All is lost.'

Word-Withus looked up. 'My friend, this is why I have come, to usher in the air of life for every Doing to breathe. Always remember: Nothing is impossible for the Builder.'

Years passed and Word-Withus's fame spread, and the miracles increased as Word-Withus continued to reflect the Builder's loving nature and power. The Special Doings plotted to get rid of him, and the scorpion arranged assassinations, but all the attempts on Word-Withus's life failed.

Then, early one morning on a stream bank where the blades of grass and field flowers wore dew like crowns of sparkling diamonds, Tender Storm ruffled Word-Withus's hair and whispered into his heart, 'The time is approaching.' The leaves on a nearby bush drooped at the anguish in her soft voice. 'The time for you to enter into and implode the Doings' awful blindness with your light, so that they may breathe and see.'

Gooseflesh rose on Word-Withus's arms and traveled down his spine. The suffering that he would soon endure was too awful to be imagined, too hideous to be considered. He had pushed it from his mind all his life, leaving it for its time so that he could stay sane.

Chapter 11

Papa Builder's heart ached for his son, who was so much part of him that he was him - but yet was also separate. He prepared a gift to encourage Word-Withus.

Tender Storm brought him a message the next day. He was to climb to the peak of one of the high mountains in the district, together with three of his closest, most trusted students.

The group was dripping perspiration when they reached the summit, so when a thick, extraordinarily white cloud floated around them in a breeze of delightful coolness, they laughed for joy until they became aware of another sound.

A rumble, soft at first, emanated from the cloud as if the waves of the sea had somehow reached the peak. Word-Withus, who had long since felt the Builder's manifested presence, began to glow as if he were the sun, and then brighter than the sun. Dazzling rays of light shot from him like bolts of lightning, sizzling the air. The three students dropped to their knees on the rocky peak in fearful worship.

With heads buried in their arms, they

realized that the rumble was increasing. It almost sounded like a voice - it was a voice! Terrified, they glanced up between their fingers. Their teacher was so dazzling that they could hardly see him. He was surrounded by the Sentences, also glowing in white glory, but not nearly as brightly.

One of the students whisper-gasped, 'We must make memorials here for Word-Withus and the Sentences.' Before he finished speaking the cloud thundered, 'Word-Withus is my beloved son. Honor and listen to him, not the Sentences, for he reflects me better than they do!'

It was from the re-telling of this event that the Doing students coined the expression 'thunder-struck', for the power of the voice from the cloud knocked them flat.

After this Word-Withus's admirers recognized that he was somehow connected to the Builder, and they followed him in still greater numbers. They even threw their coats and jackets on the dusty roads so that his feet would not get dusty. Word-Withus's heart pounded to rhythms of both dread and expectation of joy, knowing his time was approaching.

It was in this period that Word-Withus was honored by an invitation to dinner at a Special Doing's house, much to everyone's surprise. Tender Storm brushed by his cheek, whispering 'yes.' Word-Withus accepted. But when he arrived at the mansion, the servants acted as if he weren't welcome. It was as if the SD regretted making the offer, or had changed his mind.

The other guests had their desert-dusty feet washed and patted dry so that they would feel refreshed for the evening meal. Expensive oil was rubbed over their hot, perspiring scalps. But Word-Withus's feet and head were conspicuously overlooked. All through the many courses he was similarly insulted, his food served last or peremptorily removed before he finished eating.

Just before dessert was brought from the kitchen, a woman who had been hired to dance for the guests' entertainment suddenly flung herself at Word-Withus's feet, her overflowing eyes smudging her heavy stage eye-makeup.

There was much speculation, afterwards, about her identity. Some said she was a local prostitute, others were sure she was a notorious adulteress from the next village. One thought he remembered seeing her at a recent gathering of Doings who listened to Word-Withus teach in the square; perhaps she had been healed there, or forgiven. Or maybe, being near him during the evening, she had simply caught her first glimpse of the love that shone from Word-Withus's soft brown eyes.

Whatever the reason, there she was kneeling at Word-Withus's dusty feet and actually washing them with her tears. The guests were appalled!

Worse was to come. She did the unthinkable by removing her headscarf so that she could use her hair, her very long loosened hair, to dry Word-Withus's skin. Every Doing knew that a woman who uncovered her head in public was making a statement about her lack of morals.

'You can't imagine - she rubbed *her* hair over *his* hairy toes! And between them! And over his dry, rough soles. Let me tell you, I wanted to throw up,' said one of guests afterwards in a local pub. 'And there's worse. My friends, the cheap thing then started kissing his feet, and she wouldn't stop! She was slobbering all over them, anointing them with oil and kissing them!

'What about Word-Withus? What did he do?' asked a listener, his ears flapping.

The raconteur shook his head. It was almost too much to tell and expect to be believed.

'He turned to the SD and told him a story about two guys who owed money to a loan-shark. One owed him twenty dollars and the other owed five hundred. Then the shark lets both guys off the hook. Ha! Wish I knew one like that! Anyway, Word-Withus asks the SD, "So who would love the loan shark more?" Of course, the SD says, "The one who owed the most and got let off the hook." "Exactly," says Word-Withus. "You get forgiven a lot, you love a lot back. The less you accept forgiveness, the less you love. That's what we're seeing here, tonight." Folks, it's like he was saying that the creature crawling around under the table was better than the SD!'

The pub rocked with raucous laughter as tankards were lifted and banged on the counter and tables. But one patron slipped out into the darkness and made his way along the dry, stony street until he came to a well encircled by a low wall. He sat there in the soft moonlight and thought about what he'd heard while the lightest of zephyrs swirled around him, unnoticed. After a while he dropped his head and whispered, 'Thank you, Builder, sir. I believe I am precious to you, though after all I've done I don't know how that's possible!' His shriveled, hurting heart expanded out of its constricting armor of I-am-notness like a dehydrated pea tossed into warm water; he walked home whistling a tune under his breath, happy for the first time, and quite unaware of the glow already pouring out the unlocked windows of his heart and surrounding him in a halo of light.

The next day the Special Doings were more desperate than ever to find something that would turn the populace against Word-Withus. Until then they couldn't lay a hand on him, for the Doings would rise up in protest. The SDs followed Word-Withus everywhere, searching his speeches and actions and asking him tricky questions to catch him out, but to no avail - until one evening the Special Doings were handed exactly what they needed, gift-wrapped and ready for use. It happened like this:

Word-Withus was again at dinner, this time among friends. He was increasingly aware that he would soon, very soon, experience at the Doings' hands the worst death they could conceive of inflicting upon him.

Also seated at the table was a young lady who had been deeply affected by Word-Withus's teachings. Some said later that it was the same girl, now grown up, whom Word-Withus had long ago saved from death by stoning. Others thought she was someone he had healed. There was speculation that she was the cleaned-up version of the SD's dancer. Whoever she was, she noticed the faraway look that crossed his face during the meal, and sensed his tension.

No one noticed her leave, and all were still eating when she returned a little later. Concealed in the voluminous material of her robe she carried a carved marble flask of perfumed ointment that was almost beyond price. It was her dowry from her wealthy father, meant to be sold when she married and so provide for all her needs for the remainder of her life.

She walked softly across the flagstone floor, her clothing swishing around her, and stopped behind Word-Withus. Then, raising her arms, she smashed the marble jar's neck against a jutting corner of wall and poured the costly ointment over him.

The guests gasped as the magnificent scent wafted up their noses. The aroma was impossibly delicious, a fragrance that reminded each one of a wonderful memory from his or her past and made the pleasure almost real enough to be re-experienced. While it lingered in the air everyone was happy; but afterwards, when they discussed it, opinions changed…

As the thick, aromatic liquid dripped down Word-Withus's hair and beard and soaked through his clothes to his skin, he took the woman's hand in his.

'Precious child,' he said, and this time it was *his* eyes that were in danger of overflowing. 'You have anointed me for my burial. Your gesture will be honored for all time, through all the centuries to come - not because of the price of the gift, but because you wanted to show me that I am worth everything to you, and that you trust *me* for your future provision. Little one, I thank you.'

As he spoke, a light breeze flickered candles and lifted the woman's hair. Word-Withus smiled in spite of his tears; he rose and left, followed by a trail of glistening, oily drips across the floor.

Later, behind closed doors around the town, even his friends asked angrily, 'How dare she squander so much money? And on a man who isn't her husband, or even her fiancé? What a waste! How could she? Someone should have stopped her! Who will marry her now? Nobody is worth such a price!'

When first light dawned, a figure stiff with anger stalked to the Special Doing's Office of Complaints. His name was Always Doing, and he'd been at the dinner table the night before. He was enraged about the fortune that had been spilled over Word-Withus, treating him like a god. He was enraged that Word-Withus had accepted the offering without hesitation, as if entitled to it. He was enraged because no one cared enough about him, Always Doing, to do something so beautiful for him.

The anger, jealousy and bitterness of his I-am-nots carried him to the Complaints Desk and helped him write and sign a statement with a flourish. In its pages he promised to betray Word-Withus for a fee, when an opportunity arrived.

Tender Storm relayed this information to Word-Withus, who was sitting on his favorite hilltop watching the morning sky adjust hues.

Word-Withus sighed. 'It's better so,' he said. 'I'm ready. It's time to invade their darkness so that nobody will ever again be able to separate himself from the light of our love.' His voice grew softer. 'I - we - must follow them into the hidden depths of their darkness, the places we've never experienced because we've only known goodness and light, and togetherness.' He shuddered. 'We're so part of each other, Storm. In my love for you and Papa I'd rather suffer alone – but I won't have to, though I'll *feel* desperately forsaken. That's a major necessity of the torture. But I will not, shall not, absolutely won't forget that we're in this together and that though I don't sense your presence you'll be in it with me, experiencing it just as much as I will.'

Tender Storm rushed through the surrounding bushes, whirling loose leaves into the air. 'I know, I know,' she said, her whispery voice husky with the sadness of ages, yet strong with resolve. 'But afterwards, when they discover that no matter how deeply they tunnel into evil, they will find us there waiting in their darkest depths to let them know we are still in them, loving them just as much as when they're being sweet and kind – well, it will change the quality of their lives. They'll learn that absolutely nothing they do can separate us and our love from them. Nothing, because we've already been to the pit of their darkness and even beyond!' Her smile was like a rainbow of light on a gray day. 'They're worth it,' she said, and then she was gone.

Word-Withus sat with his arms around his knees, staring over the parched land of Striving-to-Become that shimmered to the horizon in a relentless heat haze. In his imagination he saw it lush and green, and filled with laughter.

'We love them enough to do it,' he said. 'We love them enough.'

That night Word-Withus, aware that it was the last meal they would share, dined with a dozen of his closest friends. Afterwards he tore twelve hunks from a loaf of bread on the table, strewing the surface with broken pieces. The group watched the strange ritual in rapt but bewildered silence.

Word-Withus glanced from one to the other. 'My dear friends, there is something I must tell you, which will shock and distress you. By tomorrow evening my body will resemble this loaf. There won't be much left of me to recognize.'

There was an instant uproar around the table. All the Doings asked the same thing in different ways, each shouting over the other. How? Why? What? Word-Withus waited until they were quiet before continuing.

'Dearest ones, you have come to know that I am more than I seem, but this is not the time to discuss that. You will understand later. What I want to tell you now is that I came for one reason that contains many others: to restore the Builder's breath of the island of Being-by-Seeing to the Doings. This will enable you to find the Builder in yourself and all others.'

A combined gasp of shock issued from the listeners, and hope flitted brightness across their faces.

'In order to make restoration possible I have to gather all the Doings that ever were or ever will be, including you, into myself, making you all part of myself.' He raised a hand as murmurs began again. 'That brings us to my death and resurrection. Dear friends, I must die, and you will die with me' – he had to chuckle at their aghast expressions – 'but relax, you won't feel it!' He looked at each one present with almost tangible love.

'My precious friends whom I love as much as I love the Builder, I want you to always remind yourselves, with similar pieces of bread, of what I'm about to do for you, because there will be so much power in it that remembering will bring peace and joy and healing. When you eat, remember my body, broken so that you can be whole.'

After eating the bread he continued the discourse, which, though his friends didn't understand, they intuited was pregnant with meaning. He took a goblet and filled it with wine. 'When you drink wine, remember that my blood flowed to wash away the sense of separation from your body, and soul, and spirit – and especially from your dear blind eyes!'

The room was silent as death. Every troubled gaze, filled with grief and bewilderment, was fixed on Word-Withus. He thought, *I love them with all my heart, with all that I Am.* He loved them and all the Doings so much that he would do whatever was required a thousand billion times over if necessary.

'My little children, when I have completed my mission, the sense of separation you feel will be destroyed as you breathe the same pure air as Allmen and Divita did, air from someone you don't yet know. Her name is Tender Storm, and she will purify your eyes and minds and ears, enabling you to know the Builder and find him in you. For that is life, my dear friends: knowing the Builder and his abiding presence!' Then he added with a wide, enigmatic smile, '*Our* abiding presence.'

Chapter 12

The Doing disciples stared at one another, their eyebrows wiggling up and down and forward and back. Was Word-Withus saying the Wall that had stood for thousands of years really wasn't there and never had been? It was preposterous! And that bit about being with the Builder, inside them, what did he mean?

One of the men, part of the group that had followed Word-Withus from the beginning of his ministry, whispered back behind his hand, 'Maybe not so farfetched – at least the bit about Wall. Remember the story we heard as kids, about the Doing who worked as a servant in the scorpion's palace, and stole a golden goblet encrusted with jewels? His neighbor, who was envious of his position, told him a lie about Big-Ego sending out his guards to chop off the man's arm and other hand.

'Even though it was just a tall tale, the man thought it was true; he left his house and family and possessions and hid in a cave in the mountains for the rest of his life. They found his bones only last year. Even if what we believe is untrue, even if it's crazy, if we believe it it's very, very real to us.' He chuckled softly and added, 'Like the monsters under the bed our children are petrified of!'

Word-Withus, who had paused for a sip of water, glanced warmly at the friend who had backed him - as if he had heard him - before he spoke again. 'The true core of all religion is a set of rules telling you what you must do to please, or draw closer, to some or other deity. That is how you have mistakenly chosen to interpret the Sentences. I pray that, having heard my words, you will instead have eyes to see the Builder in you, as he is in me. And to see yourselves in me, and me in you and us in him.' He looked earnestly from one to the other. 'This is what I came for.'

A mighty smile spread over his face and he stood, his arms upraised, as if what he foresaw was too magnificent to be spoken of while seated. 'When my task is finished,' he said, his voice hoarse with emotion, 'you will live in the fullness of union and relationship in and with the plural One who is all in all!'

He may as well have been speaking an unknown language. His friends stared at his intense face in perplexity.

At last, breaking the bewildered silence, a hesitant voice spoke from the far end of the table. 'Excuse me for interrupting, sir, but what about, you know -'. He lowered his voice in fear and took a breath. 'What about Big-Ego, the scorpion?' There, it was out, the question they were all longing to ask. In their blindness they hadn't understood most of Word-Withus's words anyway...

A smile chased the clouds from Word-Withus's face. 'Ah, yes, Big-Ego. Well now, how would you feel if I told you that he's about to be stripped of all his strength and power and authority? Because that's the truth!'

There was bedlam around the table. Someone stood on his hands, others shouted. People in the street looked up to see the cause of the noise. Word-Withus raised a hand for order.

'The Scorpion will have no power at all, but he has a persuasive tongue. Remember my words: if you listen to him he will always, and I mean always, try to get you to go back into a life of I-am-notness, desperately obeying the Sentences to earn right-standing with his version of the Builder.

'My children, I've given my life so that you can be free of the darkness that raised the non-existent Wall of Separation. From now on you will always have the ability to choose light. I beg you to choose it!'

He spoke as if the battle was already won, but like Tender Storm and Papa Builder, he knew it had hardly begun.

Later that night, Always Doing betrayed Word-Withus to the Special Doings. They immediately sent out, and accompanied, the SDPs to find and arrest him.

When Big-Ego heard that Word-Withus was in custody he sent his personal guards to help torture him. By morning Word-Withus's body had been so beaten and whipped and cut and sliced that some of his bones were exposed. His hair was pulled out by the handful. He was mangled so brutally that he could hardly be recognized as a Doing, let alone as Word-Withus. But through all the stench of blood and sweat, every so often a hint of expensive perfumed oil rose from his torn skin, reminding him of truth and purity and love, strengthening him.

Worse things still were done to him, too

terrible to tell in a story such as this. Let us rather skip over to the next section.

Moments before Word-Withus died after a savagely-prolonged agony, he cried out to Papa Builder and Tender Storm as the breath was being strangled from his lungs. Although they were inside him he felt separated from them by an infinite distance.

'Papa, Storm, it is so black here - I can't feel you! I may not be able to bear such despair!'

'We are with you, Beloved,' Tender Storm and Papa shouted in anguished unison from inside Word-Withus's heart, so loudly that the cosmos rocked and stars exploded – but they knew the darkness he was tunneling into would block his hearing. Suddenly a waft of perfumed oil drifted up from his broken skin on a wisp of wind, into Word-Withus's blood-soaked nostrils, bringing a precious reminder of love. It strengthened him to proceed deeper, like a pearl diver flexing his muscles to reach depths beyond any previously attained - depths never before comprehended by the Builder, whose experience was only of light. No shadow could withstand their glory glow; so darkness was an unknown factor, seen, yes, even clinically understood, but never experienced.

As Word-Withus descended further still into the Doings' darkness it enveloped him greedily, sucking out all hope, all remembrance of love and light and togetherness, all beauty, all trust, leaving a residue of unimaginable despair and fear and selfishness. On the surface the SDPs jeered at his writhing body as if his torment was a joke; this too increased the length of the seemingly endless downward spiraling tunnel.

At last he reached the bottom – and there he dug still farther, and when there was no way to go deeper he went deeper, again and again and again, until his mind was as broken as his body and his torment unfathomable, and once there the Builder knew that finally there was no darkness or evil or lostness or heartache or misery in the cosmos that they had not absorbed and overpowered with the light of their love. Only then did Word-Withus give his wracked body permission to die.

His remains were left to rot where the

torturers dumped them. A few of his Doing friends were courageous enough to collect the mutilated corpse, and one of them donated his private tomb so that it could be buried with a form of dignity. But the once-weekly day of rest arrived, made obligatory by the Law of the Sentences, and there was no time to honor Word-Withus's remains with sweet-smelling spices. Several of the mourning Doings, with great effort, rolled a heavy rock across the tomb to seal it, and then with tears and heartache, the brave group went home.

Big-Ego received the news of Word-Withus's death soon after it happened. He ordered a feast prepared, with dancers, and jesters, and music. As cymbals clashed and drums beat and the choir sang his praises, he smirked and belched and on one or two occasions came close to remembering again how to laugh. His huge body filled most of the ballroom as he lay on his back with his dangerous pronged tail flipping and flapping in the air. He was as close to being happy as he'd ever experienced.

The party lasted for days, and might have continued on indefinitely if not for an unexpected event. The exhausted orchestra was taking a forbidden break between songs, and the dancers grabbed the moment to rest their feet. Big-Ego raised his massive head and opened his mouth to swear at them for stopping, when suddenly the huge castle doors swung open of their own accord. Radiance poured into the dim room, but it didn't emanate from the sun. It was pulsating and cascading from Word-Withus.

Afterwards, nobody was sure how they knew it was Word-Withus, because the figure glowed with whirling, shooting shafts of brilliance that almost looked like wind-borne words hewn of burnished gold, but which were too bright to examine. The accompanying noise was like a mighty torrent rushing by in flood, or maybe a hurricane blowing at full force – a hurricane that had pulled in all the stars and nebulae and galaxies and exploding suns of the universe and was whirling them round its shining circumference. Nevertheless, the Doings recognized him - even though he was supposed to be dead, and even though he towered as high as the beams supporting the ceiling that had been built to accommodate

Big-Ego's bulk.

It was impossible! They must be dreaming - but why then was the Scorpion shuddering and shaking and whimpering and trying to scurry away as if he were as small as the cockroaches that infested his dank corridors? Why, when Word-Withus looked at him with rays streaming from his eyes like highways of light, did Big-Ego diminish, scale by scale, until he was no larger than a Doing child?

'Is that the one who terrified us all these years?' Is that Big-Ego? Why, he's so small!' 'But we thought he was powerful!' The Doings' whispers rose to a roar and with the shouts came fury at the memory of all they had suffered under the scorpion's rule. They advanced on him and would have ripped him apart if Word-Withus hadn't stepped forward.

'My children,' he said in the same quiet voice that, as always, commanded attention. Somehow it rose easily above the sound of the hurricane. 'Big-Ego lies huddled at your feet because he has been reduced to what he originally was - an object whose only power was his persuasive tongue. It is my victory, over the darkness that allowed the Wall of

Separation to rise, which has shrunk him to the size he is now. There is no need to further harm him, for the greatest hurt he can suffer has already been applied.' Word-Withus's smile was filled with a sweet sadness. 'What is that, you ask? Why, the loss of his ego! He will never again be called Big-Ego. From now on his name is De-feeted-and-Disarmed!'

As Word-Withus spoke, the little scorpion withered further into himself until he squirmed in the dust - armless, legless, tail-less. All that was left of him was a squeaking mouth, like a tiny entrance into a dark and cavernous chamber. Later on De-feeted-and-Disarmed would design a cone that turned his feeble voice into a roar, like a mouse with a megaphone. But at that moment he wanted only to scuttle away and cringe in a dark corner, for the Doing's anger had transformed into something far worse – laughter!

Word-Withus turned away from the wriggling, mouth-shaped object at his feet and walked to the enormous castle doors. They opened ahead of him. Tall as the highest oak and resplendent with light, he stood outside the castle and waited.

Before long almost the entire population of Striving-to-Become was gathered before him. Already they knew of the scorpion's defeat, for the news passed from one to the other with excited murmurings.

All were awed by the glowing person before them. Somehow it wasn't strange that he was so large, or so luminous. In fact, it seemed - right. A hush of expectation fell on the crowd, like the silence after a fanfare of trumpets though there had been no trumpets. They waited, still and eager, for Word-Withus to speak.

Afterwards, some said it was as if the words themselves formed in the shimmering air, almost visible but not quite. Others thought that Word-Withus took on the form of the words while retaining his own shape, and they couldn't explain how that was possible. All the while a light breeze kept them cool in spite of the sun's heat – a brighter sun than they had ever known.

'My children,' Word-Withus began, 'this is a new day, the beginning of a new era. Life as you have known it has ended. It may look the same, but it has changed forever - because the

Wall and its blinding power have been demolished and I have taken you, in your darkness, into myself. Look and see and know that there is nothing preventing you from stepping into a life of freedom and beauty, for the Wall and its lie of separation from the Builder are no more!'

There was a united gasp of shock that turned swiftly to joy as everyone searched the empty sky for the wall that had, until then, been ever-present, made visible by the Sentences engraved into it.

'You shall no longer be called Doings, for you are no longer Doings! I have reinstated the inheritance that Allmen handed over to the scorpion, when he as the first Being chose to become a human Doing, ever-functioning from a place of brokenness and striving. From now on you are again human Beings! You are restored to knowledge of the presence of the Builder, as Allmen and Divita were – and way more, even as the Builder always planned.'

A shout of sheer joy rose from the vast gathering.

Word-Withus continued, 'You need never strive again to earn points, or work for the

Builder's love, for now you can perceive that you have always been loved. He and his love and acceptance are in you, as is Tender Storm and as I am. In my dying and death we experienced the sum of all Doing darkness, and persevered to its extreme, until it gave way before our light. You are human Beings again!'

Another great shout of joy rose from the assembled crowd. But Word-Withus wasn't finished. He raised his hand. All became quiet.

'You are human Beings again, but one thing has changed since Allmen and Divita lived on the island of Being-and-Receiving. They were one with Builder. He filled them, his love was their nourishment and their Being. But after they believed they were not what they were and chose to *earn* their loveliness instead of being it, they were cast off the island and its life-giving air. Now it has been returned to you!' He raised a fist in victory and the crowd went wild.

'Yet,' he continued, 'you are living, not on the Island, but in the land of Striving-to-Become. From this day forward the Builders' breath and life are in you, but many of those not here, or still to come, will not know it. I repeat: the Builders' life and air is inside you. Some may look around and only see that they still live in the land of Striving-to-Become. They will need to be told that though the world looks the same, the air has changed. They will need to be told how precious and beloved they are!'

'Sir,' interrupted a bearded young man, rather cheekily, from near the front of the gathering. 'Sir, does that mean there will be no more pain or heartache, or suffering?'

'My son, it means that no pain, no suffering, will be endured alone, for we will be with you in it, feeling with you, strengthening you, loving you. When you find us there in the depths - or in the daily despair that sometimes seems as if it is all of life - sharing our love and strength and compassion with you, it will change your perspective entirely, regardless of the outcome.'

The young man seemed taken aback by the response, and perhaps a tad disappointed. Word-Withus saw a light breath of wind ruffle his hair, and smiled.

He went on speaking for a long time. Some

of the new Beings wandered off to buy some juice, not noticing a little face rolling after them that consisted mainly of a gaping little mouth. It was whispering about how long-winded Word-Withus was.

Word-Withus's last words of the day were the strangest of all. 'My precious friends,' he said, 'I must leave you now, and you won't see me again.' A great cry of dismay came from the Beings; it climbed to the sky and echoed as mournfully off the hills as a bell tolling for the dead. Word-Withus waited for the sound to subside before continuing, and everyone noticed how large his smile was; and they wondered.

'But I will not be gone!' he said, his face radiating light even more strongly. "I shall be living inside each of you, and who can see inside his own heart? Do not fear, my little ones, for though you won't see me, or Papa Builder, or Tender Storm, we will never, never, never leave you. Think of this in the day of your failures, when you feel deserted because you nose-dived and are tempted to remember the Sentences and feel justified in naming your I-am-nots. Then remind yourself that I-am-nots do not exist – we, the Builder, are the truth about you. Hear me as I say again, we never have and never will leave you.'

Joy bubbled up inside Word-Withus like a spring rising deep inside a mountain, like a river being birthed. It had been worth it! He had made his way inside the Doings' great darkness and the darkness was no longer able, and never again would be able, to silence his presence. The Beings could now rejoice in *being* cared for, *being* provided for, *being* healed, and *being* loved and loved and loved – all because they were precious to the Three-in-One-Builder, not because they had earned it by doing good behavior or doing extra prayers or doing long quiet times or doing deep studies. Some of them would perform these actions anyway – but because they were loved, not to earn that love. And if they didn't do anything, they were just as much loved.

Chapter 13

When Word-Withus finished speaking the sound of roaring wind and gushing torrents swelled to a deafening crescendo, and the light display intensified around him until it seemed it would swallow all the nights of eternity, and the air felt so thick with trembling joy and peace that it was perfectly unsurprising when it supported him as he stepped up, and up again, and still up, until he strode off into the shining mist that had formed in the sky above them.

On their way home some Beings met up with a group who had not come to the gathering, who laughed at them for listening to Word-Withus all day in the hot sun. These hot and thirsty Beings became embarrassed and decided to forget what they had heard… but afterwards they knew better, and remembered, with escalating joy.

Still others went their way deeply moved by what Word-Withus had said, but little worries crept in like ants on a picnic blanket: first just a few, but soon followed by many. The worries gnawed away at the excitement they'd felt at learning the air had changed. Nevertheless, they were haunted by Word-Withus's words, and finally they, too, believed and experienced the beauty of the new life that had been given them.

But some listened with their hearts and heard and understood everything. They went home already making plans to breathe deeper and make time to get to know the Builder whose presence was now becoming real to them. They were so excited about the new life that they could talk of nothing else. They were like people on fire with love, and they trampled on the little mouth that jabbered at them about not listening to Word-Withus, squashing it underfoot without noticing.

These new Beings, understanding what a cosmic event had taken place because of Word-Withus's life, death and resurrection, were delighted to find they didn't need to change jobs or schools to go searching for the Island of Being-by-Seeing, because it was already in them! They could breathe in fresh, glorious life with every breath.

Nor did the Beings have to worry any longer about how many scars they might earn, for they walked forever forgiven - though of course there would be consequences for their actions, good for good and bad for bad. That is simply common sense!

At first, because of the clamor and busyness of everyday life, it was a bit hard to hear Word-Withus's voice in their heart. But they soon developed inside ears, and learned to trust his gentle guidance. They learned, too, to close off De-feeted-and-Disarmed's wheedling whispers, which always tried to make them feel like failures, reminding them of all they were not, enticing them to do-to-become what they already were, just as he had tried with Allmen and Divita!

De-feeted-and-Disarmed was soon nicknamed 'The Mouth' by the most of the Beings, who laughed at his mutterings. But those who didn't understand or hadn't heard, or were not yet able to believe, that Word-Withus had made them Beings again - walking, living homes of the Builder - were terrified of the Mouth. He convinced them with his megaphone that he was as big as Big-Ego ever was. So these fearful Beings nervously put on armor every day to protect themselves from the tiny Mouth, and sent out armies to fight him instead of focusing their attention on the Builder, and believed the lies spread from this miniature source of darkness that tried to minimize the Builder's immeasurably vast, never-ending love and acceptance. The Mouth said the Builder made the Beings' children sick in order to punish them or their parents for some or other failure – thus accusing the infinitely kind and loving Builder of behavior that no human Beings would consider acceptable with regard to their children.

The Mouth even whispered that the Builder sent hurricanes and earthquakes to destroy their homes and lives as a judgment on their bad behavior – though Word-Withus had carried all judgment on his shoulders, leaving nothing to be judged.

Some Beings found they could build their own kingdoms and lord it over others by repeating and preaching the Sentences. They cajoled Beings into acting like Doings by continuing to try pleasing the Builder through obeying the Sentences' commands, instead of just accepting his love and pleasure and walking in a grand new life where the love they received flowed freely from them to others.

In fact, the lying Mouth had no remaining power at all, except what was handed him by those who believed the same old lies that he jabbered on about, sounding like a scratched gramophone record caught in a groove that forever repeated the same old lines: 'you are not worthy, you fall short, you-are-not, youarenot, youarenotyouarenot…'

The Beings who didn't know better, listened to the Mouth's nonsense instead of to Word-Withus's voice saying gently inside them, 'You are infinitely worthy, precious beyond price, eternally forgiven and loved.'

Nor were those sad Beings tuned in to the enduring shout that resounds throughout the universe like a mighty storm-wind aflame with light, vibrating in tune with the dancing stars, always ready to resonate with the Builders' presence in every heart:

'Know the truth about Our love and acceptance dwelling within even your deepest darkness, delighting in you – and live!'

AFTERWORD

My heartfelt thanks:

To Wes Yoder, my indefatigable agent who tasted potential in the dough and brought in Becky Nesbitt for baking directions from a pro; to Wm Paul Young (*The Shack*), who responded to Holy Spirit prompting and added Dr. C. Baxter Kruger (*The Shack Revisited; Patmos; Across All Worlds,* etc.) to the mix; to Baxter, master chef extraordinaire, for selfless and tireless help in kneading the unwieldy mass into shape; and to Mary Stevens, whose insights picked out many foxy little lumps.

About the author

Toronto-born novelist and ghost writer S.L. McGregor is an adventurer and globe trotter who sailed the world for seven years on a catamaran, was a missionary in Africa, an artist, restauranteur, youth pastor, and coordinator of a charity for street children in Cape Town - to name but a few. She has also church-planted in Europe, now lives between France and Italy, and is a mother. Her diverse multicultural experiences infuse and inspire her characters and books. She is passionate about remedying misperceptions regarding a loving God.

* 9 7 8 2 9 5 5 8 6 6 3 0 6 *